An Oathsworn Chronicles Prequel

The
CATACLYSM

Z.R. McCormick

THE CATACLYSM

HILLMARCH
PRESS

The Cataclysm

An Oathsworn Chronicles Prequel

Copyright © 2024 by Z.R. McCormick

Published by Hillmarch Press

HillmarchPress.com

ISBN: 978-1-966180-04-3 (ebook)

ISBN: 978-1-966180-05-0 (paperback)

ISBN: 978-1-966180-07-4 (hardcover)

Cover design by Daniel Camomile

Map design by Z.R. McCormick

CONTENTS

THE LANDS OF
ANDAAYA
REACHWIND
KEEP
HALLS OF
ETERNAL SLUMBER
HIG
BALDEIR
AUTUMNHOLD
DOR TELMO
SABRON

Calharon
Ilia
Nalindor
Ostinlaë
Vinar
Southmark
The Veil

AUTHOR'S NOTE

If this is your first time picking up *The Cataclysm*, thank you! I hope you enjoy reading it as much as I did writing it.

What began as a little experiment to explore the history of *The Oathsworn Chronicles* quickly outgrew its intent, and somehow we ended up here, with a lengthy novella bordering on something bigger. The world of Aldaria and the stories to come are shaped and deepened by so much that happens in these pages, and I can't wait to walk that journey together. But until then, the fall of Andaaya awaits you. The past that shapes the future.

If you love delving into the names and languages of the stories you read, you're in luck! Check out The Aldarian Compendium near the back for a full glossary of terms to help you out along the way.

Enjoy!

Suggested Reading Order for *The Oathsworn Chronicles*

The Cataclysm - a prequel novella

The Chase - a prequel short story

Awakening - Book One

Arrival - a companion short story

Heir - a companion short story

A Legacy of Ashes - a companion novella

The Mages' Merchant - a companion short story coming late 2026

Well of Souls - Book Two coming late 2026

THE CATACLYSM

Chapter 1

Light Among the Ruins

Ash.

Ash and smoke filled the darkened sky. No sound rose from the glade of the ancients, save the mournful crackling of flame. Warriors clad in armor of silver, blue, and gold gleaming in the pale moonlight, filed between the towering figures of nameless kings, their chiseled robes crumbling away from the mossy cliff face. The company passed wordlessly into the glade beyond. The Halls of Eternal Slumber stood for millennia, a testament to the reverence and honor bestowed upon those who wearied of life and sought rest beneath the hennaleth, the first saplings of the Elves.

A man, long in years and wisdom, stepped from the ring of warriors. Simple gray vestments rendered the mage noiseless as he approached the threshold of the vast hall. His white hair blazed with shades of red and orange as he sadly glanced upward. The massive boughs of the hennaleth that once shaded the ancestral chamber as a natural roof from their exceptional heights would shade nevermore. Faint embers sprinkled from the charred, glowing branches as if they wept at their destruction.

"The Firewalkers will pay for this," a soldier growled, stepping towards the wall where a train of polished stone chambers between marbled columns faded into the gloom. The smooth white exterior of several were rent and shattered, shards of glass littering the carven floors and glinting in the firelight. He sheathed his sword, stepping to the nearest chamber and removing his silver-mailed gauntlet. He reached inside, feeling for a pulse on the old woman pinned under the crushing stone. The old mage watched as the soldier shook his head.

"Check them all," the mage murmured.

"They have taken the iluvasil," another man replied. "Without the stones—"

"Check them all."

The warriors fanned out along each side of the corridor, examining every opening, each chamber that once held the greatest sages of Aldaria. Now all that remained of their guidance were silence and flame.

The mage walked quietly behind the searchers, recalling the names and faces of each person within. Countless elders, leaders, and friends—all dead. Taken without mercy or remorse, defenseless within this hallowed place. He studied one man still within an intact pod. His eyes were closed and relaxed above wrinkled cheeks and a grayed beard flowing to his waist. He had never woken, oblivious to the death forced upon him. The mage breathed deeply, his obsidian walking staff clicking faintly against the debris-strewn tiles as he moved further into the catacomb.

The fear-filled eyes of a woman suddenly wrenched him from his grief-stricken path. He looked upon her pale face, faintly creased with untold age, unable to tear away from her awful gaze. Her eternal slumber had ended abruptly, pulled from the paths beyond where the keenest of mind might perceive the far-off realms, perhaps catching an echo of the Creator's First Song. But there was no greeting awaiting her, no welcoming hand to release the door and usher her back to the mortal world. The dreamworld of the iluvashtin had become her tomb. A solitary tear fell from the old mage's piercing blue eyes as he forced himself to finally look away.

A faint glimmer beyond the falling embers caught his attention. He shuffled closer, moving to where one of the colossal columns supporting the ornate overhang shielding the recesses of the iluvashtin had collapsed. A massive bough from a blackened hennaleth above had plummeted into the hall, catching against the pillar and burying a section of the wall. Yet where they met, a slight opening remained. The mage knelt down, shifting the charred, slender limbs concealing the source of light.

An iluvasil.

"Here," the mage called out. Several soldiers came running, their clinking armor echoing in the cavernous room. He stepped back from the rubble and set down his rough staff. He closed his eyes, reaching out with his mind, feeling, praying for a spark of life.

Nothing.

He turned his thoughts upon the shard of iluvasil, melding the pool of its magic with his, feeling the vast reservoir of the stone open to him like brimming floodgates. He raised his hands.

The mountainous bough trembled, stirring from its deathly fall. The hall rumbled, the ruined pillar shifting as the smoldering wreckage lifted slowly into the air. With arms extended, the mage guided the branch towards the center of the passage, embers and twigs scattering across the stone. Gently, he lowered the mass towards the floor, dry branches shrieking in protest. He turned his attention to the pillar, repeating the motion and lifting the cracking monolith from the wall. Dust scattered the sparks of flame and moonlight before relenting as it settled back upon the ruin. In the dark, hopeless void, the solitary light shone brighter.

"Something at last," the first soldier breathed. He moved past the mage to inspect the pod. "No occupant, but the iluvashtin appears functional."

The mage nodded, turning to the other soldiers. "Errol, Brindan, please bring the salvage cart to the gate. I shall assist Heran in preparing it for transport." The two men disappeared into the shadows. The mage moved beside the soldier at the pod and knelt. He slid back the stone sealing the iluvasil's encasement. Suddenly, the hazy room burst with silver light. The crystal pulsed vibrantly, energy coursing through its luminous depths. It was small, hardly the width of a fingernail, yet its brilliance outshone the two larger iluvan nestled behind it. The mage reached in, uncoupling the stone from its metal spindles, and the light vanished.

"Grandmaster?" Heran whispered.

"It is enough."

Chapter 2
Nalindor

"Stop!"

Baskets tumbled across the weathered street, rattling against the stone. His firm hand groped for the signpost, the white fabric of his loose shirt flapping madly. Havarius swung around the corner, lunging between a pair of passing wagons, their horses too tired and inundated with the noises of the city to care. A moment more and he would be lost in the sea of merchants, laborers, and refugees.

"You there!" An Elf in viridian armor turned around as he caught the faint cry of the street vendor. The guard's hand moved to the slender, curving sheath of smoky glass at his side as he sidestepped a group of bystanders suddenly drawn out of their monotony.

Just my luck.

Havarius pivoted, dashing away to the left beyond a low building of white stone where a multitude of merchants clamored within its open archways. The Elf yelled again, breaking into a sprint. His inhuman speed would catch him in seconds.

He reached deep into his mind, stilling his nerves and excitement, grasping for the Current rumbling deep within his consciousness. *There*. Havarius inhaled deeply, closing his eyes only for a moment, then released. He flew through the opening of a farmer's cart, hanging carrots thumping like dull wind chimes as he passed them, untouched. Lunging up the building's outer staircase in a blur, he launched himself weightlessly across the street and onto a tiled roof beyond. The guard raced into the street, searching the crowd, before spotting a flicker of movement above. With a panicked cry, the Elf barreled through the bustling throng.

But it was too late. Havarius soared across the rooftops, the magic lifting him effortlessly as he bounded over the narrow market streets towards the upper city. Satisfied once the noise of pursuit vanished, he released the spell, dropping into another mob pressed against the edges of a square where a troupe of performers danced and bards played upon their merry instruments. Many of the onlookers clapped and cheered, immersed in the joyous event, even if only to escape for a moment the pain and terrors that ravaged their world. His feet hit the packed earth near the building, startling a pair of young ladies. They giggled, whispering quietly to each other as he adjusted his ruffled shirt, straightened his belt, and ran a hand through his long, dark hair.

"Ladies." He nodded, and they laughed once again. Then he slipped through the crowd, vanishing as a whisper.

⸺ ◈ ⸺

"You're late."

Havarius turned around, dropping his hands from the great oaken doors he had painstakingly slipped through. Apparently not quietly enough.

"I'm sorry, father, but you've seen the crowds. You can't get anywhere now without nearly being run over by a horse or pulled into some desperate performer's show." His father frowned, pulling his peppery gray beard down around his chin. Dark eyes studied him a moment longer before he resigned with a deep sigh.

"Clean up, Havarius. We leave for the palace in half an hour."

"Yes, father."

Satisfied, his father turned and disappeared into his study beyond the foyer. Havarius let out his breath and crossed the carpeted entry, passing the sweeping columns and marbled benches where his father's advisors always waited for admittance to the sequestered study. He hurried down the hall, quickly scaling the tiled stairs and heading for his room. Pulling the carved door closed, Havarius strode across the small, shadowy chamber and took the cloth pouch from his waist.

Let's hope it was worth it, he thought. He stuffed the bag behind the cushion and mound of pillows in the window seat that overlooked the sprawling city. For a moment he studied the endless blanket of white stone dotted with twisting spires of green. The ancient hennaleth dwarfed the grand Elvish structures as they stretched towards the heavens. Yet for all the city's beauty, Havarius could feel the shadow of fear that pulsed within its crowds. Not even the splendor of the Elves nor revelry of the season could conceal the sins of man.

His father was waiting in the carriage when Havarius rushed into the courtyard, tugging at the stiff collar of his embroidered tunic. He hated these formal affairs, and not just because of the clothing. He clambered into the carriage and the driver quickly set the pair of horses into the street. His father was regally dressed, a vest of gold and rich blue shrouded under his furred cloak. He gazed at the buildings, unblinking.

"Father?" Havarius murmured. His father turned, fixing his eyes on his son. Reserved determination quickly replaced his worry, but Havarius had seen it.

"Forgive me. There is much on my mind."

"The summit?"

"Yes, and more."

"Surely King Fael will support us. We've always been the Elves' ally, and with Grandmaster's evidence…"

"It is not so simple," his father said, rubbing a rough hand across his temple. "Sentiments are not enough. I fear we still lack the proof needed to convince. The Everking has kept Nalindor and his people out of this war for a century. It would take a miracle of Elowë for today to alter our fortunes."

Havarius grinned. "Then we'd better start praying." His father smiled faintly before returning his gaze to the window. The carriage creaked in their anxious silence, drawing closer to the palace.

"I must get word to your mother," said his father, breaking the pause. "I fear she and your sister are no longer safe in Reachwind Keep. The western front goes poorly. Will you bring the iluvimír to my study before dinner?"

"Yes, father. Will they join us here in Nalindor?"

"I… It would be unwise. I miss them deeply, as you do. But even here, we are not safe. Especially as I serve as ambassador to the king."

Havarius nodded. "Calharon, then?"

"Yes. The High Eldvenir still control the northern roads. It is safe, and the whole of the Order stands between it and the battle." Worry overtook his father's tired, dignified face.

"We'll find a way. To save them, and all our people," Havarius declared. His father smiled, a sad but proud smile.

"I pray that we do, my son."

⸻◆⸻

Havarius had visited the palace many times in the decades apprenticing under his father, but the sight always took his breath away. Massive hennaleth lined the wide approach. The closest ones intertwined with towering spires of polished stone, sparkling in the bright sun. The spires' carved arches wove around the woody pillars and climbed over the central dome where the Great Well pulsed within its depths. Ancient statues of dazzling warriors, graceful mages, and fearsome dragons dotted the courtyard's sides, where channels of bubbling water flowed towards the city. Each figure was breathtakingly sculpted, lifelike in nearly every way as if the Elves, humans, and dragons were watching every soul who crossed the threshold into the heart of Elvendom.

They left the carriage at the base of the looming balcony and stairwells leading to the palace. Havarius followed closely behind his father, matching his brisk pace as they strode towards its colossal gates. The chiseled stone stood open. Depictions of Elves elegantly dancing with an array of creatures from majestic eagles to noble stags adorned both sides of the grand entrance. They crossed into the hall, their eyes adjusting to the soft glow of its lamps after the brightness of the day.

"You must wait for me outside the council chambers," his father instructed as they turned down another lofty hall. Grand chandeliers of golden glass blazed along the corridor.

"Yes, father."

Beds of dazzling flowers and trellises of verdant foliage lined the passage. The sweet scents of jasmine, gardenia, and plants unknown to Havarius filled the air. Had he one of his books and a cozy nook, Havarius could have stayed there for hours, quite content.

They turned once more, coming to a small juncture where several similar halls met before a modest space with stone columns shaped in the likeness of towering oaks. At the end, a set of doors sat closed, golden lamps gently pulsing on either side.

Before them stood a man, wizened in age, leaning on his obsidian staff. Thick, white hair ran almost to his shoulders to meet his soft, ashen vestments. A short beard covered his firm jaw beneath piercing blue eyes that looked up towards them. Havarius and his father approached, bowing respectfully.

His father smiled as he rose. "Grandmaster Silvanus."

Chapter 3
Parley

Silvanus returned his smile. "Welcome, Ambassador Orian." He glanced at Havarius and nodded. "And to you, Eldvenir Stormcrown." Havarius inclined his head.

"Have the others arrived?" Orian glanced towards the doors, a frown forming beneath his beard.

"I do not believe so."

Suddenly, the door creaked, causing Havarius to jump. An Elf maiden slipped into the room. She had fair skin and flowing chestnut hair covering her gently pointed ears. Her dress was of earthen tones, vibrant greens and rich browns with hints of silver. Though simply designed, it accentuated her natural grace and beauty. She lifted her face, her startling green eyes meeting Silvanus' own.

"Welcome, Grandmaster Silvanus and Ambassador Orian," she said, joy and song whispering at the edge of her voice. "High King Fael is ready." She gestured towards the entry and veiled chamber. Orian nodded to his son before following Silvanus. The Elf silently closed the doors behind them.

Arches of stone cut in the shape of trees bending to meet one another framed the circular chamber. The trunks of four massive hennaleth divided the room into four curved sides, the lowest of their branches intermingling to form an impenetrable web over the center. A wide, round table stood there, appearing itself as a tree growing from the smooth stone floor. Its polished top glowed in the warm light of the Elvish orbs hanging from the branches by golden chains. The natural rings of its wood were perfectly sealed within the table, curving around to where the Everking sat in his oaken seat.

"Welcome, my friends," he spoke in a thrilling voice much like the attendant's. Long, raven hair flowed to meet his red robe embroidered with leaves and branches in shimmering hues of gold. Keen gray eyes gazed at them above his joyful smile. A crown of rich branches adorned his head with a trio of diamonds gleaming as if they had sprung from the crown itself.

Silvanus and Orian stepped forward, bowing before the king.

"Ma Elowë vesir nau oín," said King Fael. "May the Creator smile upon you."

"And you as well, my king," Silvanus replied, nodding. The king motioned to the seats nearest him.

"We are overjoyed by your presence, grandmaster," King Fael said as they joined him. "It is a blessing in these troubled times. I pray there were no difficulties on the road?"

"My passage was a secure and needed respite. I thank you for arranging it, and for this... meeting." The Everking's smile faded slightly.

"Oín su remon," the king replied, "most welcome. It is my hope that today brings a new dawn to our land."

Another door across from Silvanus opened, and the attendant returned. Two figures followed briskly. He glanced over, locking eyes with the imposing man, who froze, his sharp jaw clenching.

Silvanus inhaled as discreetly as he could. "Firelord Turgaen."

"Grandmaster Silvanus." Turgaen's neatly trimmed hair and beard were black as night against his fair, faintly wrinkled skin. A dark tunic with thinly embroidered patterns of gold and red enclosed his powerful chest, along with a heavy cloak of black fur.

"Welcome, Firelord Turgaen," King Fael greeted. "Ma Elowë vesir nau oín." He gestured to the seats opposite Silvanus. Turgaen paused, his amber eyes boring into Silvanus, until finally releasing their contest and moving to the Everking's side.

Silvanus looked at the second figure, his brow slightly raised. She was young and quite beautiful. Blonde hair cascaded behind with an elegant braid running down the length. Her bright hazel eyes scanned the room, studying every detail. The woman's complexion resembled the Firelord's, as did her dusky velvet gown with golden accents. Without a word, she took a seat beside Turgaen.

King Fael nodded, contemplating each of them. "We gather today, my friends, to address the future, not only of Andaaya, but Aldaria itself. In this, the Year of Remembrance, after a century of bloodshed and war, let us take council together, for the sake of peace.

"War of any kind grieves the heart of Elowë. Bitter still is the quarrel between brothers. Even now, you remain such in his eyes, and in the sight of the Elves. I urge you, friends, to remember this bond. Consider the pain this conflict brings upon your people and Andaaya. Let us reconcile and put the iniquities of old behind us. Will you join me?"

The chamber grew painfully silent. At last, Silvanus stirred. He shifted in his seat, bringing his arms to the table and leaning to meet the Everking's hopeful gaze.

"High King Fael, ever have your people been kind and generous to us, the First of Men. It was at your very feet that our ancestors learned knowledge and found our place in the Creator's Song. And when Lornan betrayed the Oath and forsook the wisdom of the Elves, we did not waver." Silvanus felt Turgaen seething, his furious eyes shooting daggers. "For centuries we prayed for reconciliation, that the pride and lust for power of Lornan's disciples would recede in his death. Yet, when the seed of corruption endured, spreading even to the Second Men, we could no longer peaceably abide. Until the Firewalkers renounce the Creed and atone for the chaos unleashed in Edros and against my people, there can be no peace."

As the immortal king's eyes softened in sadness, Silvanus turned to Turgaen's fury with his own cold resolve. Turgaen would find no weakness in the Oathsworn here. Trembling, the Firelord rose from his seat, its wooden legs faintly scraping the floor. He inhaled, anger roiling as a storm set to unleash.

"As if the Oathsworn are not guilty of the same sins," he hissed. "Pride and arrogance belonged first to you. Who protected the men of Edros when the Giant King rose? *We* did. Who risked the Wasting Plague to deliver the Elves' elixirs of lendilmyne? *We* did. Who cultivated their powers when the barbarian chieftains discovered and warred over magic? *We* did. And the Oathsworn? They hid in their palaces, buried in the wealth plundered from the eastern world, caring nothing for the plight of others."

"The Firewalkers used these same people to advance their own aims, Turgaen," Silvanus objected, rising to face him.

"*Cultivated*? Edros burns under the conquest of this archon your father raised in Hamidia. He has turned the Creator's gift into an instrument of war, killing thousands. For naught but a desire to dominate."

"We taught the clans to *survive*, Silvanus," Turgaen growled, leaning heavily on the table's gleaming surface. "The Oathsworn take comfort for granted, knowing nothing but the safety of the Elves. But out there, in the wilds, we outcasts learned long ago the one rule of Aldaria: fight, or die. Perhaps your people are finally awakening to this reality." A cold, triumphant gleam crept into Turgaen's eyes. Silvanus glared at him, gritting his teeth.

"Enough," King Fael commanded. The room dimmed, a nameless power shaking the branches in the windless air, and everyone faltered. Dread settled over every heart as Silvanus and Turgaen retreated to their seats. Slowly, the light of the orbs returned and the chamber calmed once more.

"What has been, has been," continued the king, relaxing his power. "The sins of your forefathers have shaped our world, but no longer need they define it. This is the Year of Remembrance and with it, the opportunity to alter fate hastens." The meeting stilled, growing expectant. King Fael studied Silvanus and Turgaen before he spoke. "Each celebration culminates in the final jubilation, Dragon Day. Rejoicing and reflecting on the noble sacrifice the first of Elowë's creations made in the formation of our world. And now, after a millennium of silence, the Creator has blessed me with a vision.

"Once more, the world of spirit shall merge with the world of mortals. Once more, a herald of Elowë shall proclaim over us. Once more, the Void-wing shall come." A mixture of awe and fear rose in Silvanus, unsure how to even grasp the legend becoming truth before him.

"The Void-wings, if any still exist, have not been seen in Aldaria for hundreds of years," Turgaen grumbled, jolting Silvanus from his thoughts. "Not even the lesser dragons remain."

"You presume more than you know, my friend." King Fael surveyed the assembly. "There can be no doubt. This Dragon Day shall fully exemplify its name. It is here, in the presence of the Void-wing, that the sins of the past may be forgotten. All must repent and renew their vow to uphold the Mantle, then by the mercy of Elowë, Andaaya may be healed."

Across from him, Turgaen lightly drummed a finger on the table, lost in thought. *Is it true?* wondered Silvanus. *With that power...* The frail plans he had fomented for weeks now seemed laughable. Perhaps with the Creator's Breath, there was a chance the celestial dragon could save his people. His ancestors had pledged the Oath before them, after all.

But no, they are too like the Elves. And thus, Silvanus knew the path that lay before him. He would pay the price to secure Aldaria's future, whatever it cost him. Until then, it was, as his adversary stated, simply a matter of survival. He warily eyed the Firelord, then cleared his throat.

"If the history of the Void-wings is trustworthy," Silvanus began, all attention in the noiseless chamber focusing on him, "there is much from this war that might be restored. But even they do not possess the power to return lost souls." He motioned to Orian, who drew from his vest a cloth, tattered and burned. Slowly, Orian slid the fabric into the light. Within the charred remnant, an emblem, a diamond surrounding an eight-pointed star, could still be clearly seen. King Fael's eyes widened.

"Our scouts returned from the Halls of Eternal Slumber with this," Orian explained, drawing back. "All that remains of those once hallowed grounds. Now, the smoking tomb of our forbearers."

Fury rose within Silvanus as he raised his aged hand, a finger pointed straight at Turgaen. "I name you, Firelord Turgaen, responsible for this massacre. Countless innocents, the sages of our people, butchered at the hands of your soldiers. *Do you deny it?*"

Silvanus could see his rage, the desire to engulf him in its inferno. Yet instead, the fire in his enemy's eyes extinguished, replaced by cool indifference.

"Of course I do." Turgaen turned evenly to the Everking. "Did I not proclaim such would ensue after my own soldiers reported the happenings near the hallowed glade? Does a single singed cloth condemn my people?"

King Fael was expressionless as he leaned forward, resting upon his clasped hands. Silvanus' confidence evaporated like mist before the sun. *Why does he hesitate?*

The Elvish king's eyes never left the torn symbol, ignoring the others. At length, the king sat back, an unusual weariness borne on his ageless shoulders, and sighed.

"Once more, I feel my words go unheeded. Is this the path you have chosen? To each pursue vengeance and the cruelty of war?"

"The Oathsworn shall do what we must to protect Andaaya," Silvanus solemnly replied. He folded his arms, staring hard at Turgaen.

A sneer played at the corner of the Firelord's lips. "Ever so noble. The Firewalkers are done sitting idly by as you rob our homeland and leave Edros to languish. It is time the world moved forward; the Mantle demands it. Accuse us of whatever falsities you might. It is the victor to whom history prescribes destiny."

"The atrocity of the Halls cannot stand unanswered," Orian interjected, "for the sake of every Andaayan."

King Fael shook his head, his crimson robe rippling as he drew himself up upon his throne.

"The evidence shall be weighed alongside each testimony," he said resignedly. "A delegation of my people shall investigate and judgment rendered where it is due. I have spoken." The assembly stirred as the king rose and prepared to leave.

Outrage stirred deep within Silvanus. How, when this time proof was so certainly in his favor, had his foe slipped through once more? *No.* The blood of innocents cried out for justice.

"Given what has been presented," he said, rising to face the king. King Fael raised a brow as the imperceptible depths of his eyes locked onto Silvanus. He felt Orian shudder in his seat. "It would be prudent to suspend operations of the Firewalker enclave in Nalindor until this matter is resolved."

"No!" cried the young woman beside Turgaen, clutching her seat and shaking her head furiously.

"How dare you," roared the Firelord, jumping to his feet. "You are no judge, presuming guilt where naught is proven."

The Everking raised his hands, glowering. "Peace, Firelord Turgaen." His eyes narrowed as he returned to Silvanus. "My decision stands, Grandmaster Silvanus. The truth of this matter is yet to be fully revealed, and I shall hold all parties as both innocent and suspect until such time. The peace of Nalindor *will* be maintained. As will Princess Caelia's oversight of the harborage for refugees."

The woman let out an audible sigh of relief. "Thank you, King Fael."

"I shall summon you all before the full council once our investigation is concluded," the king finished, sweeping the chamber a final time. "Më nala suilon vas basír."

With that, the Elvish king left the assembly, gliding towards the attendant as she reentered the shaded room. Turgaen grunted in satisfaction, wheeling around without as much as a second glance. The princess rose, chasing after her father's billowing cloak, and the pair vanished beyond the doors. Silvanus stood, lost and defeated, whitened knuckles gripping the end of his obsidian staff as he retrieved it. Orian placed a hand on his shoulder. Silvanus noted the grim sorrow in his friend's eyes and returned a small nod. They made their way slowly towards their own exit, where another attendant beckoned.

"A moment, if you would, Grandmaster," King Fael's voice echoed in the stillness. Silvanus halted, spinning to where the Elvish king reappeared across the room. He nodded to Orian, who slipped through the oaken doors, leaving them alone. Silvanus' staff clicked as he crossed the desolate space. Not bothering to conceal his despair, he met the Elf's gaze, surprised to find a sorrow and weariness to match his own.

"Why?"

King Fael's graceful lips curved into a gentle, sad smile. "Do you recall the Voyage of Tears?"

"Of course. The first expedition to Edros since the Great Journey. Where Elvish explorers were first murdered at the hands of barbarian men."

"Yes," the king murmured. "So faded centuries of peace and hope. The unbroken progress of the Mantle tarnished as we prepared the way for Men at Elowë's decree."

"And so, my forefathers erected the Veil, shielding Andaaya from the brokenness of the world."

"Did they?" The king wandered towards the hennaleth, running his fair hand along its rich bark with a subdued look. "I am not so certain." He turned to Silvanus. "Did our withdrawal merely grant license for sin and darkness to grow? Did it mark us as unfit to be Elowë's stewards?"

"No." Silvanus stepped towards the king. "Our peoples have always embraced our calling. We embody the Creator's light as a beacon to the world." King Fael paused again, staring into the growing shadows.

"I was there, my friend," he said, barely above a whisper. "I was there over a thousand years ago when my brothers perished at the hands of Men. When the Eldvenir sealed Andaaya. And yet, I cannot deny the truth of Turgaen's words. In some ways, the Firewalkers have upheld the Mantle where I have failed, content to forsake the wider world."

Silvanus shook his head fiercely, clanging his staff against the floor. "Absolutely not! All they have ever done is twist the truth, perverting what is good for their own gain. It is the nature they learned from Kanuh. The very reason they murdered generations of innocent Oathsworn within the Halls and concealed it." The Everking's attention snapped to Silvanus. "You know me, my friend. Why do you doubt my word?"

King Fael sighed, a momentary flicker of hurt in his expression. "Indeed, I know you, alenon. I have since your mother first held you in her arms. I do not doubt you." He glanced down, then met Silvanus' gaze once more, his firm countenance restored.

"But Nalindor must remain safe. I will not allow this civil war to tear apart what remains of my people. There have been many dark seasons to this conflict, on the part of both sides. Until the truth is fully brought into the light, I must do what is necessary to safeguard this final haven, no matter my personal misgivings."

"Then you do not deny the Firelord's ambition? His lust for power?"

King Fael closed his eyes and exhaled. "There is no answer you need from me in this."

Silvanus nodded. "What then must I do? How would you have the Oathsworn respond?"

King Fael gazed at him with a deep, tender sadness. Untold ages of burden and pain laced in that single moment.

"Humble yourself, alenon. Let the Eldvenir repent of their wrongs in this war and seek atonement at the coming of the herald of Elowë. Let *him* bring the renewal and justice you seek."

Silvanus' heart stopped as he gathered his breath. "That is something I am not sure that I can do."

Chapter 4
Old Wounds

The glass shattered against the wall of the study, and Caelia forced herself not to flinch. Wine seeped down the dark stone, forming a blood-red pool amidst the crystalline shards.

"How dare they?" Firelord Turgaen wheeled towards the long, carved desk beside her, his cloak ruffling behind him. Fury shone from his face, directed at unseen foes. She glanced away, not daring to speak, nor catch his gaze. The swirling mirror of jagged blue stone also remained silent. Dark shapes within its image shifted uncomfortably as heads turned to one another.

"It, it will take some time for the Elves to organize a response," stammered a gray-haired advisor from within the iluvimír. "We could—"

"Damn the Elves and their meddling!" Turgaen roared. The man's lips snapped together faster than a clam. "I will not allow them and this, this *distraction*, to halt our progress." He swerved back to the figures in the mirror, readying another verbal barrage.

"They upheld our innocence fairly," said Caelia, summoning every ounce of her bravery. Her father's rage rounded to face her. "King Fael even left the harborage in our charge. Surely, that is in our favor."

"For all the good it's been," Turgaen scoffed, holding back none of his contempt. "I placed you here to increase our influence, and yet, with each passing day, it seems the value of our recruiting efforts in Nalindor lessens. I expect results from you, daughter. Numbers to bolster the war effort, not weak-willed gestures and fawning before the Elves." Caelia bit her lip, afraid both to respond and to stay quiet. She knew well the displeasure aimed at her, yet she refused to be broken.

"All of my actions have been to repair the damage wrought before. The Everking's decree resulted from frayed relations, something we must address to operate freely. That goodwill will sow the seeds we need to protect our people. Even so, it remains a challenge to persuade each person to take up arms in a war that, for many, has seen more years than they have."

"I did not ask for excuses," Turgaen growled.

"More of our Ilumancers arrive at the front every day," a rough voice interjected. Caelia's brows raised at the sight of her brother's figure in the mirror, his arms folded across his midnight armor as her father's hand-wringing counselors melted further out of view. She hadn't expected him back this early. "A single mage augmented by black iluvan is worth a score of disgruntled farmers." She caught a brief glimpse of sympathy as their eyes met. Her stomach clenched.

"True," purred Turgaen, stepping towards the iluvimír. "And I have at least one advisor I can rely upon. Once again, Dragol, your success has tempered your sister's failure."

There it was. Shame's familiar specter welled inside her, but Caelia tamped it down, steeling her flushed expression as her brother struggled with a response.

"The conflict in Autumnhold will no doubt delay the Everking's delegates, perhaps for some time," Dragol offered. The Firelord frowned, shaking his head.

"This foray only risks drawing them further into the war. Something I intend to avoid."

"Then why not invest in mending our relations?" said Caelia, stepping closer to her father and the mirror. "Where friendship abounds, suspicion lessens. Let them see we are different from the generations of the past. Surely there is nothing we ought to fear?"

"You speak as the Elves do," Turgaen muttered, eyeing her coldly. "Tell me, daughter, what benefit have your days in Nalindor gained us?" She moved to speak, but he continued. "Our people have spent *centuries* as outcasts in our own homeland. Centuries plagued by distrust and the conceit lorded over us by the Elves and Oathsworn. Excluded from places of power, looked down upon as less, all because they could not see the gift offered in blood and cast us from their ranks."

"Perhaps it was a gift misused." Caelia crossed her arms as she met her father's amber stare.

"*Misunderstood*," he replied sourly. "They will never see it as it is rightly meant: a power granted to Men to fashion the world as it ought to be."

"And the black iluvan?"

"Another means to an end. What is the first tenet of the Creed?"

Caelia sighed. "Only the strong survive."

Turgaen nodded. "And so, the Firewalker Order embraces all advantages. Each plays a part in obtaining the victory we have so long deserved."

"At the cost of reconciliation?"

Her father scowled. She could sense his wrath flaring. "I will not allow the influence gained by generations of Firewalkers to be lost once more to an order of self-proclaimed heralds and their pompous lords. Our people and the tribes of Edros languish under the impotence of the accursed Oathsworn. *We* will be the ones to usher in a new era of glory. United under the Firewalker banner, the greatest empire Aldaria has ever seen will rise, one strong enough to outlast all others. And when the Oathsworn are no more, the Elves will finally see the utter weakness of the ones they entrusted the world to."

Caelia paused, staring at the floor of the study and struggling to reconcile her own place in her father's impassioned vision. Everything—her work to lift up the war refugees, her stature among her people, perhaps most deeply, her desire for her father's respect even as she loathed earning it—felt further from her grasp. Doubt crept deeper into her conscious. What even was she doing?

"See that the captain's visits to the camp remain unimpeded," Turgaen commanded. Caelia looked up, startled. He had turned away from her, facing the mirror and leaving an icy indifference hanging between them. "Whatever else you do here is of no concern to me, only that there be no further disruptions to our plans. You are dismissed, daughter."

Caelia curtsied stiffly, feeling numbed, and backed towards the door.

"Dragol, I am returning immediately," he continued. "I expect a full report of your plan for the mountain pass and an account of your voyage. I invested much in this farce. The return had better prove its worth."

Dragol's teeth gleamed in the iluvimír's reflection. "You will not be disappointed, father."

Their muffled conversation faded as Caelia trudged further from the study. Guilt and accusation hung over her, levied by her father's scornful eyes as they chased her down the passage. Tears threatened to spill, her lungs burning as she crossed the deep crimson carpet of the manor's vaulted entry and up the wide, brightly lit stairs towards the upper rooms.

She hated the feeling, hated herself for chasing his approval. Why did she even care at this point? Nothing she had ever done had lived up to his expectations, especially compared to Dragol's own passion to please him. There was nothing Dragol wouldn't do to earn their father's respect, but there were some things Caelia could never stomach. To her father, it was weakness. Failure.

She thrust open the door to her bedroom, letting it crash against the stone wall, before slamming it shut. Caelia took a deep breath, pacing across the pale rug towards the windows where the moon peeked beyond the hennaleth and spires of the city.

Elowë please, she prayed, glancing towards the waking stars. *Show me what to do.*

A dark bundle on the footstool of her bed caught her eye. Excitement mixed with relief ran like cool water over doubt's embers in her chest. At least there was one thing she knew was right, no matter what her father might say.

She grabbed the stack of folded clothes and changed quickly. With a last glance around the room, she blew out the candle beside her bed and snuck back into the hall. A few doors down, she silently slipped into another darkened room, undid the latch on the window, and vanished into the night.

CHAPTER 5
OF BLOOD AND FLOWERS

The savory aroma of roasted chicken and seasoned vegetables wafted through the doorway of the low-ceilinged kitchen. Havarius leaned against the opening to the back passage, relishing the last scrap of meat pilfered from the silver trays that cooks were frantically assembling as a trio of attendants waited anxiously to ferry them into the dining hall. Havarius could hear the din of conversation echoing from the stone corridor beyond.

Carriages bearing dozens of the Oathsworn's highest leaders began revolving through the courtyard of their manor not long after he and his father returned from the Everking's palace. It had been one of the most tense and uncomfortable rides in his life, his father lost in bitter contemplation. Grandmaster Silvanus had arrived a moment after, and the two quickly sequestered themselves in his father's study as the staff hurried about in preparation for the evening.

Havarius knew his father would be immersed in heated discussions over the war and strategy for the remainder of the night. No one would even notice his absence. He wiped his hand on a discarded cloth, then slipped into the passage. He wound his way back to the upper floor, creeping across the desolate hall and coaxing his door open. Once inside the darkened room, he ripped off his constricting garments, exchanging them for a loose tunic and cotton trousers. He sighed and stretched before striding over to his desk. Its solitary candle cast shifting shadows on the rough walls and oaken furniture. He strapped a dagger to his belt, then knelt by the pillows of the window seat. After a moment, he pulled out the pouch and tied it beside his blade, then stepped onto the seat. Brief laughter echoed in the hall and he froze, eyeing the door. Nothing.

Then he turned the small handle on the window, pushing open the iron-wrought frame with a small squeak. Havarius shimmied around the edge, stepping onto the slate tiles of the angled roof. He clambered up to the peak and turned back, drinking in the sight of the majestic city, its spires and foliage dotted with glowing lights as the faint moon peeked between clouds. He made his way to where the hall below intersected with another, and Havarius followed it towards the back of the manor. From there, he surveyed its modest gardens, bathed in gloom.

Havarius slid down to the roof's edge, catching the corner and dropping onto another section over the second floor before lowering himself onto the empty balcony of a guest room. He paused, stilling his mind and reaching for the Current. Suddenly, his legs felt firmer, as if all fatigue had melted away and his flesh replaced with iron hide. Steadying the magic's flow, he crept to the railing and vaulted over. Exhilaration rushed through him as he plummeted towards the turf. He met the ground feet first, shins vibrating, though without pain. Havarius rolled, absorbing the impact as the draw on his energy bloomed to compensate. He cut the connection, releasing the magic, and the hardened sensation in his legs dissipated.

The world was ominously silent within the tall hedges. As a child, Havarius had been terrified of the foreboding grounds, particularly at night, when the shadows seemed to lengthen with each step. Even now, the deteriorating sprawl gave him the chills. He made his way towards the dry fountain at the center. The space was empty, as desolate as the lawn beyond the hedge.

Something jabbed his shoulder.

Havarius jumped, reaching for his dagger. A woman laughed, skipping back to avoid his flailing. He gasped and relaxed his grip.

"Cae! Are you trying to scare me to death?"

"Maybe." Her soft, golden hair was pulled into a tight braid over her slender shoulder. She wore a dusky, well-fitting top with matching pants, contrasting her fair, smooth skin. Bright eyes gleamed playfully at Havarius.

"Really, Caelia, why in all of Nalindor did you pick *here*?"

She moved nearer. "Like you said, no one comes here with your mother away. It's the perfect cover."

A small grin formed as Havarius reached for her, entwining his hands behind her back. Caelia gazed at him, wrapping her arms around his shoulders. She drew close, her breath warm against his neck in the cooling air. He brought his lips to hers, melting in a long, passionate kiss. She sighed, resting her head against his as they lingered in the moment.

"Now that you say that, why haven't I thought of this before?"

Caelia giggled, shoving him lightly. The sight of her and that pure, carefree laugh were intoxicating.

"Come on. We have business to attend to, Oathsworn."

Havarius smirked, undoing the pouch at his waist. He passed it to Caelia's outstretched hand, where she carefully took it and untied the string.

"I can't believe you got them," she breathed, eyes widening.

"It wasn't easy, that's for sure." She raised a brow, and he shrugged. "Elves."

"I'm sure I can find some way to repay you," Caelia teased. Her delicate fingers extracted a single dark seed from it. The grain itself was unremarkable, a narrow, brownish shell with white stripes, not even the width of a quill tip.

"You're sure this will work?" Havarius asked. "They haven't grown in a century. Maybe more."

"It will work. I know it."

She sat down on the stone bench near the fountain, drawing out a small clay pot from underneath. She pressed the seed into its soil, just below the surface. Havarius reached for another pot and another seed. They sat, arms brushing, with the pots on their laps.

"Let's see how much you've learned," Caelia whispered, watching Havarius with excitement. He nodded nervously.

Havarius drew out his dagger, placing the edge of the blade against his palm. He paused, pulling in a breath, then drew it across his skin. Pain raced up his arm as blood trickled from the wound. Quickly, he turned his hand sideways, letting the flow sprinkle onto the soil. He could feel an unspeakable power emanating from the blood, calling to the Current stirring in his consciousness. A dark tug pulled at his attention as the blood welled, imperceptible whispers pleasing to hear, but after months under Caelia's tutelage, he knew the horrors lurking behind the corrupt spirits' honeyed tones.

With practiced effort, he pushed the murmur to his mind's edge and opened the connection to the Current, feeling its limitless energy melding with his essence and a rush unlike anything he had ever experienced. Yet instead of taking the power within himself, as the spirits urged, he redirected it back into the flow, energy coursing into the soil. While he could still feel the blood's might, he noticed a strand of his own strength seeping with it, a piece of himself taken into the dust.

Satisfied, he drew back his hand, and the connection vanished. He took a strip of cloth from his pocket, wrapping it across his trembling palm. The amount of energy he'd lost surprised him. Caelia studied Havarius, concerned, scooting closer and placing a gentle hand on his forearm. Together, they gazed at the soil, holding their breaths.

Nothing.

"You did well," Caelia murmured, meeting his disappointed look. "I'm proud of you."

"Not well enough."

Then Caelia gasped, seizing him. Havarius snapped back to the vessel. A small, green shoot broke through the black soil, rising with unnatural speed. In moments, the shoot grew into a sprout, gentle, vibrant leaves splitting from the widening stem.

"It worked. It really worked."

"Lendilmyne," Havarius whispered. Caelia nodded eagerly.

"It will take time for the flower to fully mature, but look how far it's already come! This could change everything."

"How many do we need?"

"As many as we can, though we ought to pace ourselves," Caelia said. "My contact still has to extract each one. I can begin distributing the elixirs throughout the camp, starting with the most desperate cases."

Havarius nodded. "Let's get a few more started. I'll keep an eye on them over the next couple days and let you know when they're ready."

Caelia moved the fragile plant off Havarius, placing it beside her. She drew his hands into hers, running her tender fingers along the bandage. She gazed at him with an inexpressible love, such that Havarius felt he would have fainted were he standing.

"Thank you," she murmured. "I know this—us—hasn't been easy. But right now, what you've done... *This* is how our magic should be used. How the Firewalkers can still glorify Elowë and love his world. I just have to make them see it."

"Maybe one day the Oathsworn will see it too," he added, drawing her close. "I love you, Caelia."

"I love you too."

Again, he felt the thrill of her lips, all his thoughts and desires melding with her own. Joy and blossoming hope enveloped him as he lost himself in the pureness of the moment. All that mattered was them, bound by their love within the ensconcing trees and their embrace beneath the gleaming stars.

CHAPTER 6
AS SHADOWS GROW

Silvanus watched from the veiled doorway of the balcony as the pair embraced once more. Undoubtedly, Orian knew nothing of what was transpiring.

Foolish, he thought bitterly. *The boy knows not what he trifles with.*

Silvanus had always been close to Orian Stormcrown and his family. He knew this young man, and the responsibility that one day would rest upon his shoulders, as it had his father's. Yet here he was, consorting with their enemies and practicing the forbidden magic. Silvanus felt an odd mixture of pity and conflict. He knew his responsibility under the laws of the Oathsworn, and the pain and scandal it would bring upon his dearest friend. Quietly, Silvanus retreated from the room.

With a renewed sense of his years, he made his way back to the warm halls below, conversation drifting from the half-opened doors of the dining hall.

"Ah, there you are, my friend!" Orian hurried forward and placed a hand on Silvanus' arm, gesturing towards the doorway. "Warden Karrick is ready to deliver his report from the eastern front, if you are feeling strengthened from the reprieve?"

He shook away his internal debate. "Of course, alenon. Let us join the others."

Silvanus gazed patiently at the man nervously detailing the dwindling strength of their forces. A faint sheen of sweat glimmered from the poor man's brow as he shifted before the surrounding tables, hands twitching beside his silver-threaded vest. The man pulled again at his trimmed beard.

"Last, Captain Pira has rerouted soldiers from Highwall returning to duty to reinforce the garrison at Evermont. Should the second press against Baldeira fail, as is expected, the Firewalker's next likeliest avenue to breach further north is there."

"Thank you, Warden Karrick," said Silvanus, inclining his head. Karrick bowed and stumbled towards his seat as the room quieted.

"Something is not right," declared a woman with fierce blue eyes and fiery, curled hair. The deep sapphire of her dress shimmered as she rose, surveying the others.

"Warden Sophia?" Silvanus gestured for her to continue, and she nodded curtly.

"It is clear the Firewalkers are not pressing the eastern front as strongly as they could. With the newfound power of these black iluvan, they could have easily decimated Baldeira by now. It would be a smoking wasteland, just as they have done to Autumnhold."

"You believe they are holding back?" said the man across from her, folding his great, muscled arms across his bulging tunic.

"Perhaps your example proves the point. The western front is where the gains that matter are being made, to our detriment."

"The east would provide a direct approach to Calharon," Sophia argued. "They are either fools not to press it, or there is some other plan at work."

"Many Elves travel those roads to their coastal towns," another woman added. "Perhaps they wish to avoid the risk of an accident."

"The Firewalkers avoid risk as fish do water," muttered the first man. "It is the west where their path to victory lies. The increase of these black iluvan-bolstered regiments near the pass only confirms this. They mean to take Reachwind."

The room fell ominously silent. Sophia grimaced and returned to her seat as the man rose. He cleared his throat.

"Mark my words, friends. The survival of our order rests upon Reachwind Keep. And now, knowing there will be no intervention by the Elves, what then is our hope? What can thwart both blood magic and this dark iluvan?"

"Peace, Warden-Commander Gorim," said Silvanus. "Hope still burns while even one Eldvenir remains."

"What then is our move, grandmaster?" Orian asked as Gorim relented. "How ought we face our enemy?"

Silvanus paused, a new idea leaping to his thoughts. Perhaps they might yet see within Turgaen's mind.

"In war, the fog of chaos obscures many things," he answered. "Paths unknown and unlooked for remain hidden. I believe such paths exist for us, but only if we are still enough to see."

"We cannot simply *wait* for the Firewalkers to move," Gorim scoffed. "If they gain the mountain pass, they will assuredly take the Keep."

Silvanus rose, slowly taking his place before the full council. Every head followed him. He folded his hands behind his gray robe, studying his leaders with keen, unblinking eyes.

"Within the streets of Nalindor, many talented performers may be found, in this our Year of Remembrance. Why, yesterday I happened upon one such man, an illusionist, and quite skilled by my esteem. Have you seen such artists?"

Bewilderment struck every face in the room, save Orian's smirk.

"Grandmaster?" said Gorim. "I am not sure I understand."

Silvanus waved his hand dismissively. "Many illusionists are simply mages, employing their power for wealth. True talent lies in those who either have no power or forsake it. To make others see only what you wish them to see. Such that they believe they understand all your plans, not perceiving that even your right hand knows not what the left is doing. Thus, when the trick is revealed, the foolishness born of their own making is laid bare."

Silvanus gazed around the room, waiting expectantly as furrowed brows mulled over his words.

"And what trick shall we play?" Orian called, startling the group from their musings. Silvanus smiled.

"We shall defend the pass."

"But... Isn't that what they expect us to do?" Sophia stammered.

"It is. And it is enough."

"Enough for what?" Gorim added, incredulous.

"To survive." The assembly grew deathly still. "The right hand need not, nor should not, know what the left is doing. Will you trust me in this?"

"We will," Orian declared without hesitation. Around the tables, more heads slowly nodded.

"We will," Sophia concurred. Warden-Commander Gorim scanned the room and sighed.

"We will, Grandmaster."

"You are welcome. Safe travels, Sophia," said Orian warmly, bowing before she disappeared into the carriage. He stood a moment more, watching as the last of his friends rattled away into the darkness. Then he closed the great oaken door, the latch clunking into place, and paced back to his study. Silvanus glanced up from the tome he had pulled from the shelves that lined the far wall, overflowing with similar volumes.

"They are off," Orian reported. "Each to the station determined. I pray it is enough."

"As do I. Though, there is one final role I fear must be filled," said Silvanus. Orian blinked and raised a brow. "I do not believe I have had the pleasure of visiting the third floor since I arrived in Nalindor. Would you walk with me?"

Chapter 7
The Ambassador

Havarius crept across the tiled roof towards the dormer that marked his room. The last of the carriages had left, and Havarius prayed his father had not gone searching for him yet. He cautiously slid down the side, grasping the corner of the window and vaulting back through the opening.

"Truly, it is on a roof that a man finds whether he is courageous or foolhardy. Wouldn't you agree, ambassador?"

Blast.

Havarius abashedly looked up to find Silvanus eyeing his father with a gleam. His father, however, was not amused. Orian studied Havarius with a scowl that pulled at his dark eyes and graying beard, his arms crossed.

"*Havarius.* Not only have you disrespected me by forsaking this council, you have disrespected our guests and our grandmaster himself. You are not a youth of fifty years anymore! The half-millennium bestowed on you by the Joining is not a gift to be squandered on selfish whims. There are duties you are responsible for as a member of the Oathsworn Order, and even more so as my apprentice. To have abandoned such on a night as important as this—"

"Peace, Orian," Silvanus interrupted, smiling. "I believe your reproach has achieved its aim."

"Even so, I apologize, grandmaster," Orian continued before Havarius could even open his mouth. "It is unbecoming of the Stormcrown name. I will not even ask where in Elowë's creation you have been Havarius—"

"Nor does it matter, at the present," Silvanus added. "But perhaps we may now speak of our last matter, which pertains to us all."

Havarius raised a brow. Clearly, he had missed something important. Then he remembered the kiss.

Worth it.

He stepped out of the way as Silvanus strolled towards the open window, lost in thought as he observed the quiet, darkened streets. He turned back to them, slightly tapping his staff and running a wrinkled hand down the corner of the stone wall.

"I am afraid there is one last request I must make," Silvanus began. "I do not intend to send Warden-Commander Gorim and his officers alone to face the brunt of the Firewalkers at the pass. I also will join him." He glanced at Havarius, then at Orian. "I ask that you accompany me as well."

"Gr–grandmaster," Havarius stammered, "I—"

"No, no, Eldvenir. Not you." Silvanus gazed again at Orian, sadness playing at the corners of his eyes. Orian's expression changed from fading annoyance at Havarius to shock, then acceptance.

"I would follow you anywhere, alenon."

"Father!" Havarius stepped towards him. "You, you already served! You're our ambassador to the Elves. You can't go back to war!"

"Do you think our grandmaster doesn't know this?" Orian chided him, though his look softened as he studied his son. Havarius was dumbstruck.

"But... What about me?" He glanced at his father, then at Silvanus, who waited patiently. The old mage studied Havarius with a kind look.

"You have trained under your father for many decades," Silvanus gently answered. "Always there comes the day when a man must leave his father and mother. Yet their wisdom shall never forsake you, should you hold to it."

Havarius looked at the floor, confusion and despair billowing. Alone? Left in Nalindor apart from all of his family?

"What of mother and Aria?"

"I have already spoken to them," Orian replied. "They are to leave for Calharon immediately."

"Am I to go there?" Then, silently to himself, *Separated from Caelia?*

"Eldvenir," said Silvanus, "you have been set apart for something. A role the Creator prepared before you, before your father, even before your father's father. There is no fault in his designs. As leader of our order, I ask that you take your father's place here in Nalindor, as the representative of our people. As my ambassador, as long as the need remains. Will you do this?"

Havarius was stunned. *Me? Ambassador?*

"Grandmaster, I'm honored. It's just... I've watched my father. I know the importance of this role. And I know me."

"Do you?" Silvanus narrowed his eyes, a small smile forming within his white beard. Havarius stared at him, feeling suddenly unsure. "As you said, you have watched your father. Of all our people, you know best the critical nature of our embassy here. With the wisdom imparted by your father through these long years, I am quite confident you are up to the task."

Orian gazed at his son, beaming with pride and reassurance. "He is right, Havarius. You have the training and talents that our people need." Havarius looked at him, vacillating between surprise and humility. "You can be brash and headstrong. Sometimes you shirk formalities or an occasional meeting…" Orian grinned, succeeding in drawing out an only slightly embarrassed smile. "But your heart is good. I too believe Elowë has placed you here for a reason."

Havarius sighed. "I hope it's a good one, then." He turned to Silvanus. "Very well, grandmaster. I am honored to accept this, and by your confidence in me."

Silvanus nodded, satisfied. "Thank you, Ambassador Havarius. I am sure with your assistance, together we will forge a safe and secure future for our people."

Havarius bowed, then stepped forward to shake Silvanus' hand. As he retreated, Orian approached his son, embracing him. Havarius could feel the pride and love within his powerful arms, encouraging him to press bravely into the unknown.

"A drink then!" Orian declared, releasing Havarius with a firm shake of his shoulders. "Let us toast new beginnings and the future of the Oathsworn!"

"Indeed!" Silvanus laughed. Orian strode towards the door and Havarius moved to follow, a new determination in his step.

"If I may," Silvanus added, not moving from beside the window seat. "Might I have a word with our new ambassador, alenon?"

Orian smiled. "Of course. I shall see what vintage may still be uncovered from the cellar."

His father disappeared, the sound of his boots fading down the stairs. Havarius turned to Silvanus, moving back to beside his desk. For a moment, Silvanus glanced once more out the window, the breeze rustling his aged hair as the faint scent of flowering bushes from the courtyard drifted through the opening. He looked over, studying Havarius once more.

"The ambassadorship comes with both great privilege and responsibility, as you know," Silvanus murmured. "Yet I fear yours may prove the hardest of all who ever held such."

"Grandmaster?"

Silvanus scoffed. "Please, Havarius. I am much less formal with my closest advisors. Silvanus." Havarius nodded, smirking.

"You are aware of our current impasse before High King Fael, yes? And the continuing strife with the Firewalkers of Nalindor?"

"Yes, of course, but violence is forbidden here. We aren't permitted to confront them."

"True, but you are acquainted with their efforts within the city, the refugee camp most notably, no?"

Havarius' stomach churned. "I know a little about it..."

Silvanus smiled, straightening and tapping his staff lightly against the floor. "Come, Havarius. In times as dark as these, secrets kill. If not physically, then emotionally, spiritually, or perhaps relationally. Your entanglement with Princess Caelia exposes the Oathsworn to an enormous risk."

Havarius gawked at him. "Gr–grandmaster. I, it's not what you think."

Silvanus chuckled. "Indeed? Has the locking of lips changed in significance in the past hundred years and I simply missed it?"

"I can explain."

"You need not explain, Havarius. Nor do I ask you to terminate it."

"I... What?"

"I do not doubt the love each of you holds for one another. I expect it has been professed many times. Perhaps, were Andaaya a difference place, you would already have requested her hand?" Silvanus eyed him with a knowing look.

"I, yes," Havarius admitted. "If it were a different world."

Silvanus smiled at him sadly. "I pray it were so. I truly do. Alas, it is not and so here we stand at the edge of the cliff. This precarious place from where Andaaya, nay, Aldaria itself, may either rise to new heights of the Creator's Song or fall into the darkness of Kanuh himself. And you, dear Havarius, might just hold the key."

"The key?"

"The heart of the princess." Havarius' breath caught in his throat. His muscles twitched; his fist curled. He forced himself to unclench his teeth.

"You can't ask me to betray her, grandmaster," he groaned. "To *use* her. I, she's—"

"You love her. I would not ask you to deceive her."

"Then what?" Havarius challenged.

"Be as honest as you deem fit. Firelord Turgaen knows our predicament quite well. There is nothing you may reveal knowingly or unknowingly through his daughter he does not already see. But the princess is not blind to her father's faults. She knows what will happen if the Firewalkers achieve their ultimate aim."

"What'll happen to me, you mean."

Silvanus nodded. "I have no wish to end Turgaen's life, but I *do* wish to see his power crippled. For the Firewalkers to never again threaten the peace of Andaaya and the Mantle of Stewardship. I believe to both save you and her father, Princess Caelia may be more receptive to aiding us than you presume."

"She'd be betraying her father. Caelia loves him. She loves her people."

"Undoubtedly so. Yet love is a strange thing. All I ask is that you consider this. Consider seeking her aid. Should the battle for Reachwind Keep go poorly, the fate of the world may rest on one love between Oathsworn and Firewalker."

Havarius stared at the floor, wrestling with guilt and despair. *I can't hurt her, but how can I let Silvanus and my father down?*

"You need not answer tonight, Havarius," said Silvanus gently. "There is yet time to see what comes. Now, let us join your father and celebrate this occasion."

Silvanus drifted towards the door, his staff thumping softly with each step. He glanced back at Havarius, beckoning. Havarius sighed, conflict still dominating his thoughts. But he relented and joined Silvanus, shuffling towards the warm light and clinking of glasses from the hall below.

Chapter 8
The Merit of a Man

"Havarius!"

"Huh?" Havarius glanced up, startled.

"It's spilling! Quick!"

Havarius swiped a rag from across the rickety table, nearly toppling the vial once more.

"Not that!" Caelia cried. She lunged for a small glass bottle, holding it to the edge of the rough wood and using her finger to coax the viscous trail of pale, scented liquid into it. Having saved as much of the precious extract as she could, Caelia found a small cork stopper and sealed it. Then she placed it delicately on the table and wheeled to Havarius, frustrated.

Havarius felt the color rising in his cheeks. "Sorry."

Caelia sighed. She moved closer, placing a hand on his strong shoulder as he absently sorted mounds of cloth bandages within their small wooden boxes. The commotion of many men and women drifted through the gently billowing fabric of the small tent. An occasional cry or whimper cut through the noise, a continual reminder that even amongst the gleaming structures and magnificent hennaleth, the horrors of war whispered through the streets of Nalindor.

"What's wrong?" she murmured, lightly tugging him around and forcing him to meet her anxious eyes. Havarius couldn't withstand their enthralling depths. His shoulders slumped, and he reached for her hands. They fit perfectly within his, her delicate fingers interlocking with the roughness of his own, drawing the two of them closer. Caelia leaned in, kissing him softly.

"What's wrong?"

"It's nothing," Havarius muttered. "Just a lot on my mind." He held her gaze as long as he could bear. A knot formed in his stomach, and he turned away.

Caelia pursed her lips, fighting a frown. "These past few days have been a lot. *A lot*. I am so excited for you and this new role. But I understand the pressure leadership can place on a person. You know you can talk to me, right?" Havarius froze. He knew he sounded ungrateful, callous even, considering her own duties.

"I know, I'm sorry. And you're right, sometimes I forget being a princess isn't all fancy clothes and parties." He shot her a sidelong smirk and Caelia shook her head.

"You know how I *hate* costumes. Still, it has its perks."

"Like being a glorified nurse in the dingy, backwater streets of Nalindor?"

"Ouch." Caelia poked him and scowled with feigned hurt. "This camp is far more inviting than another shouting match in the Everking's gloomy halls."

"I don't know... There were some cozy looking alcoves on the way to the council chambers."

"Really? Well, ambassadors and princesses *do* spend a lot of time at the palace." She caught his eye and grinned mischievously. He couldn't resist. Havarius left the table and drew her in, wrapping her slender form in his arms. He kissed her, savoring her skin against his. A deep laugh cut through the camp outside and they sprang apart. Caelia glanced towards the flap.

"Come on," she sighed. "We should get this batch of lendilmyne over to the other tent."

She carefully hoisted the box containing narrow vials of newly prepared elixir and pushed past the fold of fabric. Havarius grabbed a box of bandages and strode after her. As he adjusted to the bright sunlight and musty stench of the street, he nearly collided with Caelia's rigid back. He followed her gaze to the muddy crossroads near the center of the encampment where the mass of makeshift shelters and small stone buildings converged.

A trio of soldiers in dark scaled armor stood in the crossroads, surrounded by a growing group of ragged and tired-looking refugees. Each soldier wore a helmet of similarly blackened metal with steel embellishments, the designs flowing from their slender cheek plates up to the winglike crowning at the top. The tallest soldier's helm was marked with red instead of gray steel, as were the accents of his armor. He laughed, shaking the hand of a young man gazing at him with awestruck wonder.

"What's a Firewalker captain doing here, Cae?" Havarius muttered, leaning to Caelia's ear. She frowned and shook her head furiously, loose strands of her golden hair swirling.

"He's not supposed to be here today," she whispered.

"*Today*?" Caelia glanced at Havarius, worry painted on her beautiful face. Havarius continued, "King Fael forbade them from recruiting inside the camp."

She sighed. "Ask them or my father and they'll tell you it's simply 'building rapport'."

"Caelia," he growled, "you know what it is." She whirled around, eyes flashing as she gripped the box tighter.

"What do you expect me to do, Havarius? I already voiced my objection to my father. You know he doesn't listen. It was all I could do to keep control over the rest of the outreach. Or would you rather I resign and let someone like *that* oversee the camp?" She jerked her head towards the captain, who now spoke eagerly to a group of engrossed onlookers, repeatedly bringing his gloved fist into an open palm.

"No," Havarius sulked, "but I ought to report it. As the ambassador for the Oathsworn, it's my responsibility."

"And have my father find out I've been sneaking around with an Oathsworn at the same time? How do you think that will end?"

Havarius growled in frustration, narrowing his eyes at his oblivious enemy. He would have loved nothing more in that moment than to shove the man's smug look into the muddy tracks under his boots.

"Come on," Caelia muttered. "There are injured waiting. Let's just go the other way."

Hesitantly, Havarius followed as she turned away from the scene and led the way through the billowing tents and unsteady whimpers of the pained souls within.

⸻◈⸻

Havarius stared blankly at his plate, his fork rolling aimlessly beside the untouched vegetables. His father and Silvanus were deep in conversation, most of which he had ignored the entirety of the evening after his return to the manor. Orian glanced briefly at his son, worry growing on his weathered face.

When the serving staff returned to take their dishes, Havarius quickly excused himself, retreating to the solitude of the upper floor. It was his father's last night in Nalindor, his last chance to see him, to speak with him face to face. Perhaps the last time he would ever have…

No, don't think that, he told himself, pacing the width of his room. *He'll be back.*

"Havarius?"

His father's voice startled him and he whirled around. Orian shifted anxiously in the doorway. "Would you join me?"

"Of course."

Together, they returned to the brightly lit hall of the main floor and headed towards the gardens. Dread grew in Havarius as his father led them outside, and he prayed the secret crop within the hedges was not about to be discovered. Instead, Orian paused, situating himself on the stone bench beside the manor that looked over the small lawn before the gardens. He motioned for Havarius to join him. For a while, they sat there, watching the trees swaying gently in the evening breeze, the pleasant smells of greenery filling the cooling air.

"I know you are upset I am leaving," his father began. "I wish times were not what they are. I wish many things were different."

"I know," Havarius conceded after a moment. "I wish we were all together again, like it was before."

Orian nodded. "Yes, my son. I pray it is not long until that day comes once more."

"What… What if it doesn't?"

"One way or another, it will," his father answered with a hint of sadness. "It falls to us to serve as we might with the hope of seeing it, while keeping that hope within an open hand and not a closed fist."

They were quiet again, the burden weighing upon Havarius as the loneliness of the path before him set in.

"I don't know if I can do this," he admitted. "If I can be our ambassador. You're our leader, not me."

"Havarius." His father turned to him. Tender love and encouragement radiated from his face, a look Havarius had seen so many times before. That stronghold of comfort in every trial and setback. And he realized just how deeply he'd taken that rock of assurance for granted, here now where he would be parted from it, not knowing when he would see his father again.

"You are ready, my son. Elowë guided you to this moment, as he guided me before. There is so much you will accomplish for our people, for Andaaya. I know you will. And you will never be alone, not truly. I will make all the time I might to speak through the iluvimír in Reachwind Keep, should you need my advice. As I am sure Silvanus also will at every step to provide direction and counsel. There is much he can give."

Havarius nodded, anxiety growing as his exchange with Silvanus from before returned to the forefront of his thoughts.

"Father?"

"Yes, Havarius?"

"What if... what if I have to make a choice where I have to do something wrong, but it's to ultimately make something right?"

His father gazed once more at the rustling branches; all the world still, save the whisper of the leaves. He turned slowly back to his son.

"It is in his darkest moment that a man discovers the truth of who he is. Each must decide his allegiance to conscience. It is a choice only you can make."

Havarius nodded, letting his father's wisdom sink into his bones.

Suddenly the manor door creaked and Silvanus' slim figure appeared in the doorway, casting a faint silhouette on the stone path.

"It is time."

Orian nodded, and they rose to follow him inside.

A large, weathered carriage saddled with baggage stood in the courtyard, its proud steeds stamping as they awaited the long road before them into the west. Orian turned a final time to Havarius, grasping him in a firm but loving embrace. Then he stood back, still gripping his son's arm, and smiled.

"I am so proud of you, Havarius. You are about to do great things. I love you, my son."

"I love you too, Father." Havarius gulped, struggling to keep his emotions in check. Orian squeezed Havarius' arm, then climbed into the carriage.

Silvanus stepped forward, nodding to Havarius. "Thank you, Ambassador Stormcrown. I will not say goodbye, but rather, until we next meet. I expect we shall speak again quite soon."

"Until then, grandmaster," Havarius replied, bowing.

"Remember my words, Havarius," Silvanus added quietly. "Consider them, and pray for the people of Reachwind."

"I will."

With that, Silvanus made his way to where the coach waited, joining his friend in the shadows. The soldier in the driver's seat cracked the reins, and the horses started, circling the enclosure and trotting towards the gate. Havarius stood frozen on the manor steps, wavering between fear and doubt, watching as his father drifted away into the night.

He felt alone, left in the darkness with all the fears of the world unknown upon him.

Elowë, give me my father's wisdom.

Chapter 9
Reachwind Keep

Darkness. Silence. Emptiness.

There was nothing in the Void, no pulse of minds, no echoes of thoughts. Even the tiny pricks of animal life seemed withdrawn, retreating from the Current humming beneath the mountains as he cast his efforts towards them. But the Void was not just empty. It was as if the darkness itself had engulfed him, shrouding the mortal realm and thwarting his sight. Something was wrong, very wrong.

"Reachwind Keep!" the driver called. Silvanus roused himself, stretching his aching joints. He leaned towards the window, looking for a glimpse of gleaming spires of gray and streaks of green. After a moment, the line of endless forest faltered and there beyond the receding slope, he finally saw the dark turrets of the keep.

"Feels like it's been a lifetime," murmured Orian beside him.

"Indeed, though Nalindor was but a brief respite for myself. Such is the power of the Elves."

The pair watched as the carriage slowly made its way down the slopes, following the twisting road as it delved back into the forest at the base of the towering, snow-capped mountains. Before long, the leafy boughs relented, and they passed into a wide, sunny plain before the trail rose again to meet the iron gates of the keep.

Its massive walls of great stone blocks, smoothed with age and many feet thick, loomed over the carriage as they drew near. Momentary gleams of helms and spears peeped from the heights where scores of Oathsworn patrolled the encirclement, disappearing between its many towers and parapets. A grand castle rose from it all, hewn of the same smooth rock with rich carpets of vines curling among the high towers and darkened windows. On either side of the gate, long blue banners shifted in the wind. Their Oathsworn insignias—an elegant kite shield with delicate lines and runes encircling a dragon with outstretched wings—looked as if the mighty creatures were poised to take flight on the steady breeze.

The gates rumbled with the deep grating of sturdy bars retracting as they granted the weary travelers passage into the courtyards beyond. They passed under the battlements, drawing to a halt near a long, shingled stable echoing with the hubbub of hostlers and horses alike. Silvanus clambered from the coach, slowly regaining the feeling in his legs as he leaned on his staff. Soon he spied a company of soldiers in silver, gleaming armor hurrying from the gates of the castle.

"Welcome, Grandmaster!" cried Warden-Commander Gorim, jostling to a stop before him. The burly man shifted in his heavy plate armor, bowing as he could. "And welcome, Warden-Commander Orian." Gorim nodded to Orian as he joined the gathering, running a hand through his peppery hair. "I trust your journey was as uneventful as my own. The commanders are ready to begin once you have refreshed yourselves. Lieutenant Jorin will lead you to your rooms and see that your belongings are delivered." He gestured to a young man in polished mail who quickly bowed. He was thin, with a sparse chestnut beard and bright eyes.

"Thank you, Warden-Commander Gorim," Silvanus replied, "but I fear there is little time. Let us go and join the others." Gorim's eyes widened, but he said nothing. With another curt bow, the company parted, and he led the pair back towards the imposing citadel and its lofty, darkened halls.

"The sentry towers have been reinforced, and we have doubled the archers posted on the eastern side." Gorim pointed a slender stick at a large drawing laid out on the massive stone table at the center of the grand chamber.

An ornate chandelier with flameless glass orbs cast a gentle, pulsating light throughout the circular war room. An immense Oathsworn emblem was carved into the stone blocks of the far wall. Silvanus paced the opposite side of the table, studying the map of the western province with a frown. A multitude of men and women in a dazzling array of armor shifted their eyes between the two men and the table. The musty room buzzed with nervous energy, knowing here the fate of the Order might well be decided. Silvanus paused, rubbing his chin.

"What of their numbers?"

"We estimate eight thousand, mostly foot soldiers," Gorim answered. "Our scouts confirmed a number of Ilumancer regiments with a supply of black iluvan. Perhaps a five hundred strong."

"Five hundred?" Orian echoed, incredulous. "That is not even half the number that took Autumnhold. Are you certain?"

"My men have keen sight and honest tongues. Their word is true."

Orian shook his head and folded his arms over his fine linen tunic. "So few mages... Something is not right."

Silvanus gazed again at the mountain pass on the map. It was not just the numbers. It was the darkness. That shrouding haze preventing him from seeing across the Void and piercing his enemy's minds. *What is Turgaen planning?*

"Firelord Turgaen also is not present," Gorim added, as if reading his thoughts. "Our spies in Sabron confirmed he returned shortly after the peace talks in Nalindor. The crown prince is leading the charge."

Silvanus hesitated. *If Turgaen is not concealing them, then who? Has Dragol grown that strong?*

"Prince Dragol is as cunning and ruthless as his father," Silvanus finally said. "It would seem the Firewalkers have their own tricks to play."

Gorim watched him grimly. "Grandmaster?"

"Are your men prepared, Orian?"

Orian nodded. "They are moving as we speak. With the great bridge demolished, it is taking longer to ferry the canisters over the makeshift path. But they will be in place by morning."

"It is a risky move," Gorim groused. "Not only will we lose the pass, but also any hope of reclaiming the south for some time."

"It prevents the Firewalkers from breaching Reachwind and closes the western front," argued Orian, placing his hands on the table. "It will take them time to regroup and push east around the Ventari Mountains, or to shift focus to the eastern forests."

"Orian's plan is our path, should the battle go poorly," Silvanus interrupted, eyeing the pair sternly. "We shall pray Elowë grants us strength and courage enough to defend our home without its need."

Gorim bowed. "By your word, grandmaster. The last of our regiments will be in place within the pass by sundown tomorrow."

"Very well. I believe then all is prepared." Silvanus turned away from the table, surveying the room of solemn faces. He knew not which he would never see again. "Commanders, take what time is remaining to rest and regroup with your soldiers at your positions. You are dismissed."

The officers bowed quickly and left the chamber, the clanging of weapons and armor echoing loudly down the hall. As the rest streamed by, a man patiently waited, taking a step forward as the noise receded. Silvanus caught his gaze and nodded towards the doorway.

"Grandmaster." The man bowed, his mix of leather and mail jingling faintly.

"Greetings again, Captain Heran." Heran rose and took a step closer.

"My report on our progress is ready," he murmured, glancing at Gorim and Orian, still bent over the map with furrowed brows.

"I am afraid it will have to wait. Once I return from the pass, I shall meet you in the study hall. Be prepared for an abrupt change in plans."

Heran bowed once more, then slipped out of the chamber.

Silvanus slowly joined the others in the center. Gorim grunted and stepped from the table, pulling at the black beard spilling over his breastplate.

"I should see to my men," he said. "We'll head out before first light and rejoin the rest at the far end of the pass."

He nodded to Orian and Silvanus, then left the room. For a moment, the two stood in silence beside the table as the specter of battle, its unease and doubt, afflicted them. Orian was the first to shake from his thoughts.

"I could use some fresh air before turning in," he said. "Care to join me on the porch?"

Silvanus drew back from the plans. "As could I."

They left the war room in the opposite direction of the others, treading across the train of rich carpet towards the west wing of the castle. After a few turns, the hall ended at a large set of oaken doors. They moved easily on their well-oiled hinges as Orian shoved, the rays of the setting sun casting great beams across the hall. They slipped out onto a vast balcony overlooking the land of Reachwind. Beyond the empty plains nearest the keep, an endless forest trailed into the west, gently rising and falling, like a blazing sea of gold billowing in the fading light. Faint hues of red and pink gathered behind the scant clouds as the distant chirps of birds making their way home rose to their ears. Silvanus rested against the thick, curving balustrade, drinking in the last moments of tranquility. Perhaps the last this land would ever see.

"I remember my first visit to Reachwind, right after my Joining," said Orian, settling near him. "It was an evening near to this. Calm, peaceful. I remember thinking that were each as perfect as that night, no post or adventure after would ever replace its hold on me."

Silvanus smiled. "The Keep has been so for many centuries, even in my youth. I like to think it as a last grace of the ancient Elves who reveled among its forests and fields, making the pilgrimage to the Halls."

"Perhaps so."

"Yet I remember our company's first voyage to Edros," continued Silvanus with a gleam in his eye. "I do not recall signs of longing on your part."

Orian chuckled. "True, though it was not until the escape from the giants that I believe we truly met. I was a little... preoccupied at the time."

"A fair point."

They were quiet for a moment, watching as the sun sank behind the trees.

"Do you ever think of returning?" Orian said in a low voice. "To Edros?"

"Of course. To ride through the deep forests of Terestia and across the high moors of Fellinor. To drink in the chill and spray of the Ander Sea once more. So much potential, so many who still did not know us, did not fully know Elowë and his gifts to Men... It feels as if a distant dream now."

"It was real. For us both."

Silvanus hummed in agreement. "Yet with each passing year of this war, the prospect of my return fades. I fear by its end that chance will have passed beyond my strength."

"I feel its end hastening," murmured Orian. "In my bones, I feel it is close. One way or the other. Perhaps it is this Year of Remembrance, or Fael's prophecy. Could it be the Void-wing truly does alter the fate of Aldaria?"

Silvanus paused; his wrinkled face, expressionless. "Perhaps."

The last sliver of sun reached the horizon, darkness chasing away the dying light and transforming the rosy skies to a dusky blue. Silvanus shifted, watching the first of the stars glimmering high above. Orian straightened and turned towards him.

"Will you promise me something, alenon?"

Silvanus met his serious gaze. "Of course, my friend."

Orian hesitated, running his hand aimlessly along the weathered stone.

"There is no guarantee of what tomorrow holds. Should something happen to me—"

"Alenon, you are among the most skilled of the Eldvenir," Silvanus interjected. "We need not linger in fear—"

"Still, I feel I must ask. Should this battle be my last, please, watch over my family. See that Lina and Aria remain safe, and that Havarius is protected. He is in the greatest danger, even in Nalindor. And there is so much he has yet to learn."

Silvanus moved closer, grasping Orian's trembling shoulders and fixing his eyes upon him. Orian's pleading gaze bore into him.

"Please, Silvanus."

"Orian, my dear Orian," he murmured. "All these long centuries have you and I stood together. There is no friend to whom a greater debt is owed nor bond of brotherhood shared."

Tears formed in the corners of Orian's eyes as Silvanus fought to restrain his own.

"I swear before Elowë, upon my Oath before you, alenon. As long as I breathe, there shall always be a Stormcrown. Your family shall be my family, and there is nothing I shall not do for you or them."

Orian gripped his arms as he nodded shakily.

"Thank you, Silvanus," he whispered, releasing his hold and collapsing against the rail once more. "Whatever the Creator holds, I can face tomorrow knowing this. And it will be my honor to do so alongside you once more."

Silvanus smiled. "It shall not be our last adventure, alenon. Let it be the dawn of our greatest story yet."

They stood side by side, resolved to face whatever lay beyond the growing darkness as the stillness of night enveloped them and the stars of heaven danced above the cares of men far below.

CHAPTER 10
FIRE AND SNOW

Bitter wind stung his cheeks as Silvanus urged his horse forward, its ears flat against its skull in obvious displeasure. The gentle warmth of the plains seemed a lifetime away, though it had only been a few hours since the group ascended into the pass dividing the Ventari Mountains into its eastern and western ranges. Yet the colossal mountains were unforgiving and treacherous, especially at this time of year. The snow had grown quickly once they had crossed the great chasm by a makeshift path since the bridge had been demolished to slow the Firewalkers' advance.

The wind howled above their chilled helms, whipping the fine flakes into an obscuring cloud. Narrowing his eyes against the storm, Silvanus could just make out the next set of watchtowers dug into opposite walls of the wide, rocky clearing. The archers on their heights shifted and stamped their feet, battling the fierce cold and winds as well as they could.

"How much farther?" Silvanus called over the buffeting winds. The captain leading the group turned around on his horse, pulling down the cloth covering his mouth and neck.

"We're in the middle of the pass, sir," he shouted. "The winds should lessen as we descend towards Warden-Commander Gorim's position. Another thirty minutes or so."

"My men are up there," Orian added loudly as he rode up next to Silvanus. He pointed towards a cleft on the eastern side, hundreds of feet above them. Silvanus could just make out a narrow, twisting path from the floor of the pass up the cliff face leading to the heights. Between the drifting snow and distance, the soldiers were completely hidden from view. "They set the canisters beneath that peak, and the peak directly across from it. At this height, they'll do what we need and more, once the iluvan sparks are triggered." Silvanus nodded, squinting as a powerful gust tore across the desolate ground.

The company continued on in silence, heads bowed against the cold. Slowly, Silvanus noticed the wind begin to abate, exchanging its furious blasts for a steady breeze. The whirlwind of snow dissipated, settling in mounds along the sides of the ravine as it sloped back towards the earth. Silvanus straightened in his saddle, releasing the stream of energy he had been using to shield his immediate group from the bitterest of the freezing air.

Then he heard it. The faint ring of steel and cries of men.

"They're in the pass!" Orian bellowed. The troop spurred the horses, quickening the pace while navigating the rough, snow-covered slope. As they neared a turn in the cliffs, another sentry tower sprang into view, its handful of archers clustered near the far side and frantically releasing volleys beyond the range of sight. Silvanus tore around the corner of the cliff, and the din of battle slammed into him with deafening fury. Hundreds of Oathsworn were locked in a furious clash, their gleaming swords and spears echoing off the stone. Beyond them, a mass of soldiers in variegated armor swarmed forward, forcing themselves upon the wall of defenders. Flashes of light exploded, spells of flame and ice bursting over the swarm of heads. Cries of anger and anguish split the air.

"Hold the line! Hold!" Gorim boomed over the tumult. He was perched on a boulder near the edge of the horde, his battleaxe waving furiously above his head. The sentries in the tower nearest him released another volley into the attackers. A new chorus of screams rose as the line faltered, giving the Oathsworn a moment to press the advantage. Silvanus slipped off his horse and strode towards the commander as the others rushed towards the center of the battle.

"Gorim," Silvanus cried. After a moment, the warrior spotted him and descended, hurrying as he could in his massive, gleaming armor.

"Grandmaster," Gorim replied, breathing hard. "Advance troops. Arrived just as we were getting into position. Our scouts must've been captured or killed; we had no warning."

"Ilumancers?"

"No, sir. Sappers. Commoners."

Silvanus growled. "Refugees baited with lies. I thought we had addressed that problem."

"Expect more! And the mages are likely to be ensconced within each unit."

Silvanus reached out with his consciousness, feeling the Current roiling like the sea within the chaos of the mountain. This near the battle, the wall of darkness was weaker, and he could sense the life force and emotions of hundreds of souls smothering the unseen world around him. He sifted through the madness, searching for reactions to his touch beyond his fellow Oathsworn.

"None yet," Silvanus replied. "Though I cannot see beyond the battlefield."

Gorim nodded. "Nor I. Might and magic are holding them for now, but more are sure to come."

"Sophia's regiment was not far behind us. We must buy a little more time."

"Aye!" Gorim spun around, charging into the line of men.

Silvanus followed more cautiously, stretching in his polished scale and leather armor as he acclimated to the fit. He paused behind the other men, who pressed against one another for a view of the front line, where the ringing of blades and gusts of spells rose above the clamor. Silvanus stilled his mind, reaching again for the spark of magic.

"Press on," he cried as an invisible force reverberated through the ranks. "Press on! For Andaaya!"

The men around him stood taller, their nerves and exhaustion lessening. A great cry rose from the Oathsworn, defiant and proud, as his wave of arcane energy infused them with courage. Suddenly the standstill shifted, the roar from the ranks of gleaming shields and helms drowning out the peal of battle. The tide surged forward, pushing the invaders back, and they faltered, their confusion mounting as momentum built among the Oathsworn. A torrent of rushing wind and ice crashed into the attackers' ranks, splintering their rough shields and slicing through their worn, patchwork armor. Many cried out and fell, wounded by the deadly spears. The enemy's resolve broke, and they turned, retreating desperately from the emboldened mages and swordsmen bearing down upon them. Another deafening cheer rose from the ranks, the taste of victory at hand.

"Look out!"

A massive boulder of molten rock smashed into the cliff side, showering the defenders with shards and snow. Men shrieked, several silenced as the stone crushed the row nearest to the wall. Silvanus cut the spell, sighing as the magic claimed its due. His mind reached for one of the blue iluvan concealed in the lining of his belt, transferring just enough energy to bolster his stamina and steady himself.

"Firewalkers!" yelled an archer above.

A new line of enemies marched around the bend in the distance, rows of gleaming scale like a sheet of midnight. Tall, menacing spears rose from their ranks, enclosed by wide steel shields. The panicked sappers halted, melding into the oncoming force and its girth swelled until they filled the pass from one end to the other.

A single shout rose from their ranks, answered by a dazzling volley as it sailed from their depths and into the sky.

"Cover!"

Oathsworn crouched beneath tall shields and summoned slabs of protective rock as the flaming darts hurtled to the earth. Silvanus raised his own wall, protecting the men around him. Arrows rained like an earsplitting storm, snow hissing in the flames. Men screamed. The soldiers near him edged closer to the center of the makeshift shield. Silvanus flicked his hand, shoving the rock back into the earth and they stood to face the Firewalkers, the field quickly shrinking.

A torrent of arrows flew from the sentry towers in response, and the Firewalkers raised their own steel and earthen shields. Suddenly, another flaming boulder erupted from the back of the horde, sailing over Silvanus' head. It slammed into one tower with a thunderous blast, smoke and snow engulfing the wreckage as it crumbled.

A fierce battle cry rose from the Firewalkers and their march became a sprint, rushing to meet the recovering Oathsworn. The defenders in the front lowered their razor spears, death awaiting any who dared approach. Silvanus' breath caught in his throat; the world frozen in silence.

It begins.

Spears and armor clashed, cries exploding as armies collided. Chaos overtook the desolation. Silvanus searched for Orian and Gorim as more soldiers rushed forward, struggling to beat back the attackers' ferocity. He spied Orian not far away, shouting as a group of Oathsworn unleashed a wave of fire on a swarm of Firewalkers. The first pair took the brunt, howling in agony as flames enveloped them. Suddenly, a gust of ice shot through the flames and a cloud of steam billowed over the surrounding skirmish. Silvanus strode forward, twirling his obsidian staff to grip it like a sword. He slid his fingers down its slender length, channeling the flow of magic through his limbs. The staff shimmered as its dark, rock-like metal reformed into a keen, gleaming edge. The knob of swirling white and black at its top twisted into a solid cross guard, and he raised the blade, catching Orian's attention. He jostled his way through the defenders swarming towards the Firewalkers, stumbling next to his friend.

"We have to destroy that weapon," Orian bellowed, barely audible above the din.

Silvanus nodded. "It and its Ilumancers are near the end of their formation, towards the southern flank."

"Can you get a group of us onto that cliff?" Orian gestured towards a wide, sloping ledge running nearly the length of the battlefield high above.

"Yes."

"Are you sure?"

"I have strength enough," Silvanus replied. "Quickly!"

They turned back towards the clash, Orian hollering at the men nearest him. The small group pulled back from the fight and more shining blades and glowing flames replaced them.

Hidden in the chaos of the throng, they crowded against the rocky wall near an outcropping, shielding them further from view. Silvanus stepped back, reaching for the Current and tapping into his iluvan reserve once more. Orian and the men huddled closer. He raised a hand and the ground beneath them trembled. Snow shook free of the cliff face, showering the group. Suddenly they rose, the ground beneath them rumbling its way towards the sky as the earth around it convulsed. The draw on his energy was enormous. Silvanus felt his iluvan rapidly dying. He slowed the platform's ascent, bringing it to a stop just below the snowy cliff, like a bizarre square reaching out into the air.

Orian and his men scrambled up the rocky slope, rolling onto the ledge behind a squat spire of the outcropping. Silvanus glanced towards the approaching Firewalkers. So far, Orian's group seemed to have gone unnoticed. They shuffled their way further behind the Firewalker ranks, drawing to where they could get a shot at the siege engine.

"Rah!"

A fearsome cry yanked Silvanus back into the fray. He glimpsed a blur of black with a shimmer of steel racing towards him. Silvanus flowed lithely around the blade, its edge bashing against the stony ground and scattering a swirl of snow. He spread his hand, releasing a blast of wind that sent the swordsmen careening into a trio of spearmen locked in combat with more defenders.

Another shout rose beside him, and he raised his smoky blade. An axe glanced harmlessly off its imbued edge, staggering the Firewalker. Unperturbed, the man raised a hand, unleashing a cone of fire at Silvanus' chest. Silvanus flicked his free hand, batting the stream aside like splashing water. The soldier charged, blade and axe grating once more as he bore down on Silvanus' smaller frame. Silvanus bent, swiping his leg enhanced with a burst of arcane speed at his opponents' and knocking the man onto his back. Silvanus drove his blade between the scales of the soldier's armor before the breath had even been knocked from his body.

Silvanus rose, scanning for Orian in the brief respite. In the distance, he caught a gleam of metal peeping high above the swell of black. Then, a blast of fire spewed from the cliff side, racing towards the oblivious Firewalkers. A deafening boom shook the pass, and the battle lulled, heads turning to catch a glimpse of the source. Smoke billowed from behind the massive force, followed by a chorus of confused and agitated cries. A cheer rose from the Oathsworn, their boldness restored.

Silvanus gasped as a stream of arrows and fireballs raced towards the cliff. Orian and his men bolted, sprinting towards the Oathsworn line as more Firewalkers spied the group, now exposed on the ridge. The Oathsworn sentries atop the last tower released a volley towards the nearest attackers, providing a flash of cover as the Firewalkers scrambled. Suddenly, a jagged lump of stone from the enemy ranks slammed into the ledge. A shower of rock and snow tumbled from the heights, sucking one man down with it, shrieking. Orian and the others dashed madly for the safety moments away. The Oathsworn around Silvanus bellowed again, roused by their comrades' act of bravery. They surged forward, shoving into the ranks of distracted

Firewalkers and sowing a moment of turmoil. Silvanus breathed a sigh of relief as Orian and the rest staggered behind the wall, clambering towards the raised slab.

Silvanus reached again for his store of energy, hastily lowering the massive platform and exhausting another of his iluvan. Orian stumbled off, panting hard and leaning on his knees. Silvanus rushed forward, patting his friend's shoulder.

"Well done, alenon! Well done."

"Thanks to you," Orian rasped, staggering to face him.

Gorim appeared from the writhing sea of silver and black, his axe covered with grime.

"Bloody good show, warden-commander," he bellowed. "Now is our chance." He raised his weapon, circling to address the soldiers surrounding them. "Push, Eldvenir! Make them regret every step! Reachwind is ours!" Gorim jostled his way back into the fray, swallowed by the mass of steel.

Silvanus traced the path to his energy, expanding his senses to touch the minds around him. Once more, his unseen presence whispered courage and fearlessness into his comrades' weary thoughts.

"This day is ours, brothers! To victory, Oathsworn! Rise and claim it!"

The throng cried out with terrible strength, crashing upon the Firewalker ranks with renewed vigor. Bit by bit, the field shifted, each step pushing the swarm of midnight scale farther down the slope. Pained shouts and the peal of blades filled the air, beaten only by the roar of defiant Oathsworn. Silvanus could feel doubt rising in the enemy ranks, the cusp of triumph at hand.

Fire, wicked and awful in its red glare, rose from the front like a terrible wave.

It loomed above the valiant defenders, blotting out the entire pass. It smote the Oathsworn, striking their ranks as a viper, greedily devouring men and arms alike in its inferno. The thunderous blast amplified the screams caught in its blaze, carrying the sweltering heat and smell of charred flesh to Silvanus as he froze in horror. The Oathsworn faltered, confused and terrified, as the fire wave vanished, leaving a field of burnt corpses and glassy stone like a patch of death at the center of the snowy field.

"Blood and black iluvan," Orian gasped beside him as he held his shield higher.

Through the gap, Silvanus could see a row of Firewalker mages adorned in armor emblazoned with streaks of red. Each one held only a small dagger, blood dripping from their palms. Menacing, jet-black tips of black iluvan poked from behind each where the large shards had been secured to their backs.

Again, the dark mages raised their bleeding hands, a curtain of fire erupting from the barren earth. The blinding wave contracted, swirling into a tight cone at the center of the battlefield. Suddenly, the blaze sprung from the earth, rocketing towards the remaining tower. Arrows in mid-flight vanished in the blaze, swallowed by the tempest. In a moment the sentries were gone, the sturdy defenses blasted away like leaves before an autumn storm.

The Oathsworn cried out, unleashing a barrage of elements. For a moment, the enemy paused, ensconced behind arcane barriers as waves of fire and ice pelted the line. The defenders marched forward, seizing the moment.

Then, a second row of blood mages sprang forward, unleashing a new torrent of fire and swallowing more soldiers in its blaze. Men howled in agony as others rushed to erect barriers and cut off the inferno. Silvanus threw his consciousness towards a pair of mages at the edge, stabbing at their concentration and the shields around their minds. They stopped, shuddering under his might, and the flames faltered. Silvanus watched as Gorim and his group unleashed a whirlwind of ice, quenching the fire and blanketing the pass in a cloud of vapor. One of the mage's barriers crumbled and Silvanus rushed into his mind, crushing his thoughts. He felt the man's life force reel as he severed his connection to the blood. The man's arrogance vanished, replaced by terror and darkness. Then, nothing. The mage crumpled to the ground, lifeless.

As the second convulsed under his attack, the other mages searched frantically for the source. He knew he was running out of time. He blasted the man's defenses apart, the curtain of emotions and memory unable to thwart centuries of skill. Silvanus encircled the man's consciousness, feeling the fear whispering through his hurried thoughts. Then Silvanus felt another presence pressing against his own.

They had found him.

Like a vice, Silvanus choked the man's mind, and he toppled to the ground, unconscious. Silvanus retreated, shrouding his thoughts in darkness and obscuring the Void around him. Momentarily free, he turned to Orian.

"Retreat," he panted. "We must regroup."

Orian nodded. "Fall back!" he cried, raising his sword. "To the peak! Fall back!"

Silvanus heard Gorim and the other captains take up the call. With hurried steps, the Oathsworn pulled away, huddling together as the Firewalkers regrouped and prepared to march. Silvanus could still sense the Black Ilumancers scouring for his presence, their deathly power enhanced by the cursed shards. But even their power could not outmatch his affinity for the

Void. As the battalion drew further away from their attackers and the churning Current of the battlefield, Silvanus felt a new presence further up the mountain.

We are here, Sophia's voice rang in his mind. *The trap is set.*

CHAPTER 11
SACRIFICE

Horns blared from the towers as the beaten Oathsworn plodded past rows of pointed barricades and scores of clean, gleaming shields. The howling storm had abated somewhat, making the mountain peak marginally more hospitable. Silvanus trudged slowly near the rear, transferring what little reserve of energy he could spare into the stragglers. Beyond the defenses, the wounded were transferred onto small wagons and ferried towards Reachwind Keep in the plains below.

Silvanus caught sight of Sophia's blazing hair; her helm tucked underneath an arm as she shouted orders to a swarm of captains near the highest tower. He made his way towards her through lines of men carrying blades, and quick-footed scouts, weaving between other warriors who stamped their feet in the cold. Gorim and Orian shouldered through the throng to join them.

"Grandmaster," Sophia breathed. "We feared the worst."

"It was a valiant effort," he murmured. "Many gave the greatest sacrifice of all on that field. We shall ensure it was not in vain."

Sophia nodded. "Yes, sir."

"Black iluvan is bad enough," Gorim growled, "but mixed with *blood magic*? These Black Ilumancers are nearly unstoppable!"

"Nearly, but not invincible," Orian countered. "We must concentrate our most skilled Void mages on each one in turn. Our combined strength stands a chance to overwhelm their minds."

"Yes," Silvanus agreed. "They are our highest priority. The other mages shall falter once their leaders are no more."

Gorim grunted. "I'll see to it." He hurried off towards the rows of anxious soldiers huddled against the cold.

"What of the prince?" Sophia asked, grasping her sword hilt with her free hand.

Silvanus shook his head. "I have not sensed him."

"Nor I," Orian added. "Defeating his blood mages may draw him out."

A burst of horns drew Silvanus' gaze back down the mountain pass.

"They are here."

Sophia slipped on her helm and unsheathed her blade, marching towards the center of the pass.

"To arms, soldiers," she cried. "For Reachwind!"

The army roared in reply, armor clanging above the howl of the wind as they rushed into position. Orian placed a hand on Silvanus' shoulder.

"To glory."

Silvanus nodded. "Creator, grant us strength."

Together they strode forward, joining the defenders crowded around the barricades. The faint march of boots echoed up the pass, growing in volume. After a moment, Silvanus spied the line of midnight scale and gleaming spears trudging through the snow. He reached a tentative strand across the Void, scanning for the blood mages. Nothing yet.

The Firewalkers stomped closer. Then, when they were nearly within bowshot, the menacing line stopped.

Silence.

Armies glared at one another across the wintry field, wind whipping banners and stinging faces as it howled across the forsaken peaks. Silvanus studied the line warily, enduring the agonizing wait as fear mixed with anticipation.

Is this where our fate is set? Elowë, do you see us?

A shout rose from the Firewalkers, fearless and filled with hate. The Oathsworn thundered back, rattling shields and swords as the Firewalkers charged. Silvanus watched, dread rising.

"Now," Sophia yelled.

A rain of arrows, black against the gray sky, streamed across the field with lightning speed upon the wind. The Firewalkers slowed, raising shields and arcane barriers. Shrieks rose and figures fell lifeless into the snow, swallowed under the feet of their companions as they charged on. Another volley poured from the towers as fireballs and arrows sprang haphazardly from the attackers. Oathsworn ducked behind the defenses, scorch marks and shafts pelting the walls.

Suddenly, the ground trembled. A boulder erupted from the ground along the far side of the Firewalker ranks, fire licking around its edges. It sailed through the air, slamming into the nearest tower and tearing a gaping hole through its side. An archer at the top lost his footing, flailing over the upper wall and crashing into the ground far below.

"Another engine?" Orian shouted, dismayed.

"No, Ilumancers!" Silvanus called. He pointed to the source, where a group of the mages in red and black armor leapt past the crater to rejoin the ranks.

I see them! Gorim growled in Silvanus' mind, catching his eye from the opposite barricade.

As Silvanus reached across the Void towards the enemy, he was aware of several other minds converging through the Current. As the ranks of Firewalkers crashed upon the barricades, the battle in the unseen realm collided, blood mages bolstered by black iluvan clashing with a score of Oathsworn as the magic of the world roiled under their struggle. Silvanus rushed to aid one woman caught as a Firewalker cracked her frazzled thoughts, penetrating her inner mind. Silvanus' presence overwhelmed the distracted attacker, catching him off-guard. Together, the pair pressed the advantage, collapsing the Firewalker's own mind. Across the chaos of the battlefield, his body tumbled into the snow. Silvanus glimpsed another Firewalker fall near the first. Suddenly, the warrior next to Silvanus gasped, staggering to his knees. Silvanus searched desperately for the man's mind, lost in the swirl of emotions and shouting thoughts in the Void.

Where are you? Eldvenir!

"Master," the man sputtered. He slumped to the ground.

No.

Another Oathsworn near Gorim fell, unconscious.

They're too strong, came Gorim's voice.

Another meteor of flames slammed into the tower near Silvanus, shaking the earth. Its top exploded, archers vanishing in the blaze as stone and wood disintegrated, pelting the defenders with debris. Silvanus retreated from the fray in the Void, raising an arcane barrier just as a chunk of stone plummeted towards his barricade. The rock crumbled as it slammed into his shield, pieces sliding into the snow around him.

Anger burned inside Silvanus, stoked by despair. *No. Not here.*

His mind raced back into the Void, slamming into the oblivious presence of a Firewalker mage. In a rage, he tore through the man's unprepared defenses, extinguishing his life in a heartbeat. His explosion of power shone like a beacon as the Current swelled, other Black Ilumancers pouncing to overtake him. A barrage of blows hammered against his wall of rage, still shielding him from their onslaught—for the moment. He returned the volley in kind, blasting another's focus apart, and the attacker fell. More Oathsworn joined the fray, stabbing with their thoughts from behind as the Firewalkers infused more of their power into the attack on Silvanus. Another Firewalker fell, crushed under his consuming will. After what seemed both an eternity and momentary flash, the barrage ended, any remaining Firewalkers retreating back into the darkness at the edges of the Void.

Silvanus looked across the battlefield, counting the unmoving Firewalkers in their emblazoned armor dotting the ground between the onrushing horde. He paused, lingering on the scattering of fallen Oathsworn behind the barricades as panicked companions shook their lifeless bodies.

Their Void mages are gone, Gorim reported from across the field. *Any of those Black Ilumancers left have retreated further into the ranks.*

There may be others, Silvanus replied. *Be on guard.*

As if inciting fate, a new group of Firewalkers broke from the main body. Silvanus watched as they reached for the earth, a fissure splitting across the stone and snow. The front line of Firewalkers pulled back from the barricades, leaving behind heaps of armored corpses, both silver and black. Silvanus leapt back into the Void, racing for the mages' minds. Unlike the others, Silvanus collided with a solid wall of thought, hard as iron.

You were saying? Gorim dryly growled.

They have embraced the Old Way, Silvanus observed.

He could only watch in horror as another molten shell rumbled into the sky. It slammed into the barricades, ripping apart a string of defenses as it sent Oathsworn flying or crushed them under its mass. Howls of delight rose from the Firewalkers as they charged the exposed defenders once more.

"Pull back to the second line," Sophia yelled from somewhere behind him.

Oathsworn scrambled to retreat from the wreckage, Firewalkers bearing down upon them as a hail of arrows and fire spewed from their ranks. Silvanus heard men cry out in agony behind him before they collapsed in the frigid snow, forever silenced.

As the last of the stragglers came through, Oathsworn mages erected more stone barriers, blocking the paths through the next line of barbed barricades before the Firewalkers could assail them. Blasts and the clash of steel rang against the mountainside and from where defenders' spears jabbed at the approaching attackers.

Silvanus hurried over to where Sophia and Orian huddled behind a large cleft, shouting over the din of battle.

"Focus the sharpshooters on the new group of Ilumancers," Orian said, exasperated. "Are there mages stationed on this line of towers?"

"Some of my best ice casters are up there," replied Sophia. "They'll find a way to take them down."

"The barriers won't hold long," Gorim yelled, dashing around the corner. "Get ready for a brawl!"

"Your men are in place?" said Sophia more softly, staring at Orian. He nodded, and she turned to Gorim. "Warden-Commander?"

"Once they've breached the line, our forces must draw the enemy to this point," he directed, "but without giving ground too quickly."

"I wouldn't dream of it," she growled.

The pair nodded to Orian and Silvanus and slipped around the rock, back towards the front lines.

"I'll join the men and wait for your signal," said Orian.

"Be careful," Silvanus warned. Orian walked towards the narrow trail up to the peak, trudging through the deep drifts of snow along the cliff side. Silvanus paused a moment more, catching his breath as blasts of spells and shouts echoed through the pass. Then he stepped from the shelter, the wind whipping across his snow-flecked beard.

A faint throbbing whispered on the breeze, barely at the edge of hearing. Silvanus froze. The clamor of battle dimmed as he focused. The rhythmic beats continued, slowly but steadily growing louder. All at once, Silvanus felt the obscuring darkness in the Void drawing closer, his range of perception to beyond the Firewalker ranks rapidly being pushed back. The hairs on his neck stood up.

No. It cannot be.

Silvanus scanned the skies.

The beating grew louder. The Oathsworn near him now heard it, glancing around in nervous confusion.

A piercing roar shook the mountaintop, amplified by the wintry wind.

It cannot be.

A dark shape broke from the gloomy clouds, hurtling towards the battle. The figure widened, limbs snaking from its bulging core.

Not limbs. Wings.

Another roar thundered across the battlefield, paralyzing the soldiers as they gaped in horrified wonder.

"*Dragon!*"

Silvanus stared, speechless, as the beast roared again, plummeting with incredible speed. Ashy, dark scales covered the dragon from snout to tail, shimmering in the faint light. Its long, snake-like neck strained towards the battle, white teeth as long as daggers bared in fury. Massive, gleaming claws flexed at the ends of the four stubbly legs pressed tightly against its underside. Seconds from the field, Silvanus locked with its blood-red eyes, its pupils narrowed slits whispering death.

Only then did Silvanus notice the figure in black and gold saddled on the creature's back.

Dragol.

The dragon roared; a gush of flames tinged with blue around its maw blanketing the terrified Oathsworn. Men screamed as the blur raced past, then ascended into the sky before mages and archers could react.

"Brace!" Gorim bellowed.

But the dragon did not circle back upon the battle. It angled to the south; its piercing eyes locked onto...

Orian!

The beast roared again, sailing towards the summit like a flash of lightning. The mountain trembled as its monumental weight slammed into the ground. Snow exploded from the peak, obscuring the cliffs in a cloud of white. Shouts of terror drifted from beyond the line of sight. Gorim and a detachment of Oathsworn sprinted in Silvanus' direction.

"No!" Silvanus raised his hand. "See to the Ilumancers. Prepare the trap. I will go."

"Grandmaster!" Gorim gaped at him, his battleaxe trembling.

"That is an order, warden-commander. This battle is yours to command."

"Sir."

They doubled back towards the battle as a fresh round of shouts from the reinvigorated Firewalkers drowned out the rest of the clamor. Silvanus swerved back towards the cliff side trail, running as fast as his bones would carry him.

He could hear the beast bellowing and men howling as he neared the top, flashes of orange and gusts of snow spilling over the edge. As he stumbled onto the wide, snowy field, he barely had time to register the sight as a mighty tail, thick as a tree trunk, lashed towards him. Silvanus ducked, narrowly avoiding being smacked off the mountainside. The dragon growled, focused on a group of Oathsworn stabbing vainly at its bobbing neck. It lunged towards them, snapping its vicious jaws a hairsbreadth from one soldier as he leapt into the snow. The others jumped to protect him, jabbing at its eyes and it reared, roaring in fury.

Suddenly, it unfurled its massive, dusky wings, lashing the air and whisking the snow into a whirlwind. The soldiers stumbled, covering their faces from the stinging frost. The dragon struck again, snapping one man in its vice-like jaws. He screamed and flailed vainly as its teeth punctured his armor. It snatched a second man in the claws of its forearm and launched itself into the air before anyone could react. It shot off across the battlefield, dropping a lifeless body into the writhing battle far below.

Struggling to recompose himself and shed the weight of darkness suffocating his mind, Silvanus surveyed the mountaintop. A clang of steel near the spire of stone at the far end quickly drew his attention. It was there he finally spied Orian, locked in a blazing battle with the dragon's rider. Orian's blade sped through the whirling snow, ringing against Prince Dragol's shimmering sword. With his other hand, Dragol unleashed a blast of flame, ripping Orian's shield from his side, sending the smoking lump crashing into a rock.

"Orian!"

Silvanus sprinted towards his friend, ignoring the handful of others recovering from the rampaging dragon. The winged terror cried out from somewhere in the distance, but Silvanus paid no attention. Another gush of flame punched Orian in the chest and he grunted, stumbling to his knees. Silvanus howled, unleashing a blast of wind towards Dragol. The prince swerved around and stretched out his hand, his barrier barely diverting the tempest. It slammed into the rocky cliff behind him, showering the field with a plume of snow.

"Silvanus," Dragol growled. His dark eyes narrowed and his lip curled as the prince studied him. Flecks of snow encrusted the tips of his dark beard, where his black and gold helm left it exposed.

"Dragol," Silvanus barked. "How dare you invade our lands. How dare you blaspheme the Creator and enslave one of the Bound!"

Prince Dragol sneered at him. "You are weak, Eldvenir. Not you, not even the dragons, can withstand my new power. With our black iluvan and dragon might, all of Aldaria will be ours!"

"Fool! You do not comprehend what you are playing with."

"And *you* do?" retorted Dragol. "Do you realize how far I have gone to reach this moment? I have sailed beyond the world's edge for this, and see how I have been rewarded!"

The dragon roared again, closer. Silvanus was dimly aware of the suffocating darkness in the Void drawing closer. It was then that he realized the source. *Not just the dragon. It is their bond, born in blood. The legends are true.*

"My power will *finally* end this war," Dragol crowed. "And neither a feeble Elvish king nor his Void-wing will save you."

"We shall see," growled Silvanus, "but your victory is not today."

Prince Dragol scowled. "Prepare to die, Oathsworn."

Silvanus raised his obsidian sword. The beat of the dragon's wings grew louder. The prince faced Silvanus, silent, unmoving.

Suddenly, the dragon flew from behind the peak, curving over the jagged tip and angling straight for him. It opened its jaws, ready to swallow him whole. With a burst of magic, Silvanus dodged to the side, the air vibrating as massive teeth snapped shut. Outraged, the dragon whipped past, circling around towards the field.

Dragol yelled, launching towards Silvanus. A fireball rocketed towards him, Silvanus narrowly deflecting it into an embankment of snow that hissed savagely. Their blades clashed, the impact drowning out the howl of the wind. Behind him, the dragon collided with the ground, shaking the earth as it charged towards the duel.

Orian leapt before the dragon, blocking the path.

"No Orian," Silvanus shouted, struggling against Dragol's blade.

"Take the prince. We'll handle the beast!" The remaining Oathsworn rallied to their commander, encircling the massive monster. It snarled defiantly, snapping at their spears and whipping its tail to keep their barbs at bay. Orian unleashed a hail of ice at its wings, puncturing several holes in the soft, velvety flesh. The dragon howled, pulling its wings tighter, its snake-like eyes blazing.

Silvanus forced his gaze back to Dragol. The prince scowled, shoving their blades apart. Another fount of flame sprang towards Silvanus. With breathtaking speed, he tore a slab of stone from the earth; the fire bursting against it. He launched the rock at Dragol, who deftly evaded it. Silvanus rushed towards him, striking with his blade while stabbing his consciousness towards the prince through the Void. The darkness devoured his attack, shrouding Dragol's mind from view, and Silvanus pulled back.

A contest of arms, then.

The dragon bellowed angrily as Dragol swung again at Silvanus. He parried, shoving Dragol's blade from his side. The prince drew back, clenching his fist. The earth trembled between them, cracks splitting the ground as the snow boiled. A gush of molten earth exploded into the air, heat blasting against Silvanus' flesh. Along the inside of the prince's gauntlet, he caught a jet-black gleam in the firelight.

Black iluvan.

The volcano gushed towards Silvanus as he retreated and sparked a connection to his remaining iluvan. Silvanus rocketed into the air atop a pillar of stone, the molten flow crashing against its base. He stretched out his hands, unleashing a torrent of ice colder than the farthest reaches of the world over the flames, chilling them into a glassy sea of obsidian. Dragol growled and raised his hand, fingers pointed straight at Silvanus. Blue light crackled at the tips. Silvanus shoved the pillar down, plummeting towards the earth just as a blinding stream of lightning whisked over his head. The massive storm crackled across the sky, spreading in every direction. A man screamed somewhere behind Silvanus as the heat of the dragon's breath wafted over him.

Dragol pointed again as Silvanus rolled behind the magma mound. Chunks of the hardened lump shattered as lightning hammered the far side. Silvanus rose, releasing his own stream of lightning towards the prince. An arcane barrier wrapped around the prince, the glowing streaks swirling like a ball of agitated serpents before dissipating. Another man cried out as the dull ring of steel echoed against the dragon's scales.

Suddenly, a pained howl split the air. Silvanus glanced at the dragon across the rocky space, its neck thrashing violently. A silver mass flew from its jaws, slamming into the earth.

"No!" Dragol screamed. The Void's consuming darkness vanished like a puff of smoke in the wind.

Silvanus watched as the dark dragon toppled, the rage within its blood-red eyes extinguished. It collapsed in the snow, sending a wave of powder into the air. He scanned the field but could not make out Orian from the straggling soldiers through the haze. He jerked back to Dragol. Wrath blazed in the prince's expression as he wheeled on Silvanus. Prince Dragol raised his hand, lightning crackling.

Except now, the Void was free, sprawling before the elder mage like a beckoning friend. Silvanus stabbed across the unseen realm at Dragol's mind, slamming into his mental barrier with enough force to stagger him in the physical world.

The prince raised again to strike him. But the distraction had been enough. Silvanus grasped the last energy of his iluvan, dropping his sword and raising both hands. The remaining shards of the magma flow exploded, launching towards the prince like a wave of razors. Dragol twitched, grasping for his barrier. Glistening shards ricocheted off the shield, but not before a handful tore through his scaled arms and legs, splinters of his sleeves flying as bloody streaks formed across naked flesh. Dragol yelped, falling to his knees.

Silvanus retrieved his sword and leapt over the rubble, striding towards him. The prince rubbed his arms, then glared at Silvanus as he staggered to his feet.

"This isn't over, Oathsworn!"

Dragol ripped the black iluvan dangling from his gauntlet, grasping it in his palm. Its sharp edge cut into him, blood seeping behind the crystal. Instinctively, Silvanus launched into the Void towards Dragol, but not fast enough. The wounds on the prince's legs vanished as skin knitted together into pinkish scars. With inhuman speed, Dragol sped towards the cliff, launching himself over the edge. Silvanus rushed after him, peering at the battle raging below. Dragol pounded down the mountainside, small craters forming as he leapt in death-defying bounds down the rock face towards the sea of Firewalkers, bolstered by his blood magic. Silvanus sighed, stumbling against a mound of boulders as weariness overtook his body.

Orian.

Silvanus turned away from the peak, hurrying towards the looming, scaled corpse where a handful of survivors stumbled about. As he drew near, he glanced briefly at the dragon, blood gushing from one of its eye sockets and staining the snow. A sheet of red was slowly expanding beneath its chest. Then he noticed the men were huddling near a gleaming silver form atop the snow.

"Orian..." Silvanus gasped, dropping beside him. Orian's plate was punctured in several spots, blood flowing freely through the holes. Grime and spit covered him, his face lacerated with cuts and fresh bruises.

"Alenon," he mumbled, his eyes fluttering.

"Hold on, Orian." Silvanus placed his hands over the bloodiest wounds, breathing hard as energy poured from his body and into his friend. The flow of blood slowed, but continued trickling across his rent armor. Silvanus' vision flickered as he spent all the energy he could muster. He toppled backwards, gasping.

"We tried, grandmaster," one of the others stammered.

"We must get him to the healers," Silvanus panted.

"No, my friend," Orian said weakly. "It is over."

"I will not leave you!"

"You must, Silvanus," he murmured. "Elowë beckons, and someone must remain to spring the trap."

Silvanus glanced towards the far end of the peak, where a small slope led to the stockpile of metallic canisters linked to a sparking iluvan device, still nestled in the fissure overlooking the battlefield.

"You cannot," Silvanus objected.

"This is my duty. Save our people. Save my family, alenon. Please."

Tears stung Silvanus' flesh as they met the frigid air. He gripped Orian's hand, breathing shakily.

"Ma Elowë vesir nau oín, alenon," Silvanus whispered. "Until next we meet."

Orian smiled, love and gratitude outshining his pain, outlasting death's whisper at his ear. He squeezed Silvanus' hand, sighing before dropping his hand back into the snow.

"Go," he wheezed. "Get my men to safety."

Silvanus nodded, stumbling to his feet. He looked at the others. "Quickly."

He glanced back as the group hurried towards the cliff, agony burning in his chest as the last glimpse of his friend atop the swirling snow disappeared. Sorrow and despair threatened to overtake him. It was as if a piece of his soul had been ripped from him, centuries of his identity sacrificed atop this accursed mountain. His breaths came in ragged gulps, stifling the grief burning in his heart.

Grandmaster! came Gorim's frantic cry across the Void. *What happened? Where is the dragon? We cannot hold them much longer.*

It is defeated, he replied numbly. *Call the retreat. It is time.*

Silvanus could sense the questions burning in him, but Gorim remained silent.

As Silvanus and the others staggered onto the floor of the pass, the core of the Oathsworn forces came rushing past. Burned, bleeding faces covered in fear ignored them, hurrying by as angry shouts and blasts echoed from behind.

"Grandmaster," Gorim shouted, rushing over. Sophia was right on his heels. "We must move! The barriers won't hold the Firewalkers for long. Where is Orian?"

"He... has chosen the ultimate sacrifice," Silvanus answered, barely audible. Then, before they could respond, "Come, we must go."

They joined the throng, rushing down the slope towards the plains of Reachwind in the distance. The soldiers were silent save for the clamor of armor and stomp of boots, exhaustion overtaking their mortal frames.

Now, Silvanus called. He felt Orian's relief across the Void.

I will look for you at the gates of the City, he gently whispered. *Can you see it, alenon? The towers framed in light. It is beautiful.*

Silvanus stopped, turning as weary men and women trudged heedlessly past.

A blinding flash exploded from the peak, followed by a shockwave that shook the very roots of the mountain, sending the defenders stumbling as snow and wind rushed upon them. The earth rumbled violently as the mountaintop vanished, an avalanche of snow and rock swallowing the horde of Firewalkers just as they glimpsed at Reachwind. The tremors continued as the cascade flowed over the corpses of Oathsworn and Firewalkers alike, consuming the trail of battle as a greedy torrent until nothing remained of the southern pass but silence.

Silvanus fell to his knees and wept.

CHAPTER 12
PETITIONS

Havarius rushed into the council chamber, flustered. He smoothed his embroidered tunic, bowing hastily before High King Fael, who sat patiently on his carven throne, a gentle gleam in his eyes.

"My sincerest apologies, my lord," Havarius gasped. "The revelries beyond the gates waylaid my carriage."

King Fael smiled and nodded, his raven hair flowing across his shoulders. "Peace, Ambassador Stormcrown," said the king with a hint of mirth. "As Dragon Day draws near, it is to be expected. It is a most joyous time, and should be celebrated as such." He gestured to the open seat opposite him. An array of Elves in marvelous robes of every hue surrounded the polished wood table. Among so many of the elder race, Havarius felt conspicuously inept.

Then he spotted a cascade of familiar bright blond hair with intricate braids in the chair nearest his. While still anxious, his deepest doubts abated. He slid into his oaken seat, forcing himself not to gaze at Caelia. The Everking inclined his head once more as Havarius joined the group.

"I have summoned you both before the council to address a most urgent matter," King Fael began, his joyful voice turning solemn. "I pray, Princess Caelia and Ambassador Havarius, your influence may address this problem."

"Of course," Caelia said respectfully. "I am certain even with our differences, the Oathsworn agree that our alliances with your people are of the utmost importance." Havarius noted several councilors' nodding in approval.

Clearly, she knows how to play a crowd, he thought.

"Thank you, Princess Caelia," King Fael replied. "As you know, we have undertaken the inquiry into the tragedy within the Halls of Eternal Slumber. Our most experienced mages were set to make the journey west to the ancient glade. However, the escalation in hostilities near Reachwind Pass has impeded my peoples' travels. They are unable to find safe passage through the fields of Autumnhold."

"Autumnhold is under Firewalker control," said Havarius. "While there are still many Oathsworn citizens in the area, we no longer have the means to communicate with them."

"I would contest that statement," Caelia argued, glancing at Havarius. "We know many Oathsworn spies are still moving through Autumnhold." Havarius glared at her, unsure whether she was serious or toying with him.

"Peace, my friends," King Fael interjected, raising a hand from his shimmering crimson robe. "There have been enough arguments between your fathers in these halls. Let us find a different path today.

"To your point, ambassador, yes, it is officially in the hands of the Firewalkers. But its proximity to clashes in the Ventari

Mountains has stoked suspicions in the local regiments. To Princess Caelia's point, many have been detained under charges of espionage—even some of my own kin."

Caelia shifted nervously, bringing the velvet sleeves of her amber dress onto the table. "High King Fael, I will personally see any Elves interned are released immediately. Please, if you have any names, I will contact the officers responsible before this day is over."

"That is unnecessary, my lady, as the matter is already being handled. But I thank you for the gesture," King Fael said. "No, what I seek is a waning of hostilities near Reachwind Pass. I am aware it has become the greatest flash point in this conflict, but it now affects my people to a degree I cannot ignore. I ask that as representatives of your orders, you present my appeal to Firelord Turgaen and Grandmaster Silvanus, respectively, requesting a truce to allow safe passage through those lands."

Havarius and Caelia glanced at each other, mulling over how best to respond. The only sound in the lofty chamber was the faint rustling of hennaleth branches, their wide, vibrant leaves dancing in the light. A woman in a rich, emerald dress to the left of Havarius leaned forward and caught the king's eye.

"If I may, avanuil," she began with a light but firm voice.

The Everking gestured for her to proceed. "Please, Councilor Livanya."

She nodded respectfully before turning her attention to the pair. Elegant strands of auburn hair wove behind her pointed ears, gathering in a perfect bun at the back. Her pale, unblemished skin accentuated her angular face, but most striking were the piercing, ice-blue eyes that bore into Havarius as if his very thoughts were known. She studied him a moment more before relenting.

"This war has affected us all, from the Halls in the west to the shores of the east. Even my people of Ostinlaë feel the specter looming over Andaaya." Livanya's stoic expression softened. "I see the doubt in your eyes, young mortals, but take heart. Should your influence succeed, the hope of a greater peace draws closer for us all. Surely that is a goal worthy of all effort?"

"Of course, councilor," Havarius conceded. He could feel Caelia watching him. "I am willing to bring the high king's appeal before my order. If the representative of the Firewalkers likewise concurs." A fleeting grin played at the corner of Caelia's delicate lips. She regarded him with confidence, eyes flashing.

"I concur. As princess of the Firewalkers, I will implore my father for a reprieve, for the sake of our steadfast allies." She dipped her head to the Elvish king. Havarius glimpsed the ease with which Caelia maintained her noble, graceful presence, even amongst the highest of the Elvish lords. For a moment, he was in awe of her beauty and dignity, humbled by the secret affection she lavished upon him.

"Allovan'oín," said King Fael, beaming. "I am certain Elowë shall think with your mind and speak by your lips. The council shall pray favor upon you and wait eagerly for your word."

The Everking rose from his throne, surveying the assembly a final time. "Më nala suilon vas basír, Princess Caelia. Ambassador Havarius." With a hopeful nod, King Fael left the chamber, flanked by several of the councilors. A low murmur grew as those left whispered among themselves, all ignoring the two humans except Councilor Livanya. The councilor rose and bowed slightly to them, then silently swept past the doorway after the king. Havarius stood and stretched, angling towards the other door from where he had entered.

"Would you walk with me, ambassador?" a sweet but serious voice called from behind. He turned to face Caelia, her brow raised and a playful gleam in her hazel eyes. "So that we might... coordinate our imminent conversations?"

Havarius stifled a smirk. "Of course, my lady."

They slipped away from the council, following the lush halls towards the palace gates. Havarius resisted the urge to clasp her hand, instead hastening their pace as the sweet fragrance of exotic flowers pressed on his senses.

"In a hurry?" Caelia teased, matching his speed.

He shrugged. "Perhaps our discussion would be best had over dinner, away from prying eyes?"

"Sounds wonderful, if I could," she sighed. Havarius stopped, shooting her a quizzical look. Caelia bit her lip, glancing down the hall before pulling him into a nearby alcove obscured on either side by thick beds of white flowered shrubs. "I have to get back to the embassy. My father is expecting a report from Dragol and I am not to miss it." Havarius frowned, sharing her obvious disappointment.

"Another time, then."

"Absolutely. I..." Caelia faltered, glancing away.

"What?" Havarius reached for her hands, bringing her captivating eyes back.

"I'm just tired of hiding *us*. You would think with everyone else gone, it would be easier, but it only makes me feel it more acutely. I wish we could reveal everything and just be done."

"I get it," he said, squeezing her hands. "I wish there was some way, too."

"My father is returning for Dragon Day in a few weeks," she added with a nervous smile.

"You're not serious."

"It's likely to be the only chance we ever get," Caelia argued. "He wouldn't dare disrupt the Elves' ceremonies. He'll probably disown and exile me, but at least by doing it then, I'll have a refuge under King Fael and finally be free of him."

Havarius gaped at her. "Putting aside the Firelord trying to roast me on the spot. *Caelia*. Do you realize what that'd mean? You're not just leaving your father and brother, but the Firewalker Order entirely. Including your work in the refugee camp."

"Of course I realize," she retorted, pulling away. "I'm willing to pay that price. For you. What about *your* cost? You could just as easily be banished from the Oathsworn."

Havarius paused. Ever since their first chance meeting, when members of both orders still volunteered in the refugee camp at the same times, he knew the risk their bond entailed. He just never dwelt long on it—which was easy when she was around. And now, with Silvanus' knowledge, his approval even...

"I would give anything for you," he replied. Caelia pressed closer, relief and hope flooding her beautiful face. "It's just... It still terrifies me." She grasped his hands once more, putting them behind her back. Havarius could feel his heart beating rapidly, pressed against the warmth of her body.

"Me too," she whispered. "But we will face it, together."

She reached up, kissing him. Worry evaporated from Havarius' mind as he was drawn into the longing of their embrace. Underneath the warm glow of the Elvish lights and aroma of the verdant passage, all that mattered was her.

Pounding footsteps shattered the silence. The lovers sprang apart, Havarius peeking cautiously around the hedge. A messenger from the Oathsworn embassy darted around the corner at the far end of the hall, racing towards the council chamber.

With a glance at Caelia still pressed into the corner of the alcove, Havarius stepped out, nearly sending the man tumbling before he reached them.

"Ambassador Stormcrown, sir!" the young courier gasped, catching himself. "A message from Reachwind. Grandmaster Silvanus requests you contact him immediately."

Havarius moved forward and nodded. "Very good, thank you."

"Shall I accompany you to the embassy?" the man added eagerly.

Havarius shook his head, almost too fiercely. "That won't be necessary. I'll be there shortly. Please go ahead, and have the iluvimír ready."

"As you say, sir."

Havarius could tell he was confused, but the man readily obeyed and strode hurriedly back down the hall. After the messenger had vanished, Havarius slipped back into the recess. Caelia hadn't moved from her hiding place in the shadows.

"I guess we both have places to be," she breathed. Havarius nodded, pursing his lips in frustration. "Meet in the garden after I'm finished with my father?"

Havarius pulled her into his arms a final time with a yearning kiss. "Definitely."

He scanned the corridor, then slipped quickly towards the exit. He glanced once more at the hidden alcove where Caelia waited for her turn, before striding towards the daylight streaming from the palace gates.

Havarius hurried into his father's study, straightening his rumpled tunic as the cloudy depths of the blue, crystalline mirror swirled patiently. He ran a hand through his dark hair, taming a loose strand as the iluvimír sprung to life, its nebulous fog spinning faster and faster as an unseen whirlpool swallowed the haze, the image of a brightly lit chamber of stone suddenly replacing it. Havarius could make out a set of arcane orbs lighting an open doorway across from the mirror, and the fading sun casting its rays through a tall bank of windows somewhere to his right. A thin man in Oathsworn mail stepped back from the other mirror, bowing slightly to Havarius before turning towards the door.

"Grandmaster Silvanus," the soldier called. "The connection is ready!"

Silvanus slowly entered the chamber. Although his bright armor was covered with dirt and grime, Silvanus appeared unharmed. Yet it was his composure that shocked Havarius. It seemed as if the weight of a thousand worlds had saddled his master since his departure. His face was ragged, his eyes lost in thought and sadness. It wasn't until Silvanus had reached the iluvimír that he looked up and met Havarius' gaze. Silvanus' expression shifted slightly, a faint gleam of relief, perhaps. Or something else?

"Havarius."

"It's good to see you, Grandmaster—I mean, Silvanus," he said, bowing.

Silvanus smiled tiredly. "You as well, my young friend. No doubt you have been eagerly awaiting word."

"Yes." Havarius stepped closer to the enchanted mirror. "How is Reachwind? Is my father there?"

Silvanus winced. "Reachwind Keep is secure, for the moment. Your father…" His voice trailed off along with his gaze. Havarius' heart dropped into his stomach. Silvanus breathed deeply, focusing back on him, overflowing with sorrow.

"Atop the highest peaks of the Ventari, the greatest terror to the Oathsworn was unleashed. A dragon from the creation of the world, enslaved by Prince Dragol's blood magic. He would have destroyed the Order. The might of Orian Stormcrown, though, proved too powerful for even the Bound to overcome. I and the Order survive only by his immeasurable courage and strength."

"He didn't leave that peak," Havarius whispered.

"No, he did not."

Havarius staggered, catching himself on the edge of his father's massive desk. His vision flickered, tears brimming in the corners of his eyes. He couldn't breathe, couldn't think.

No, he thought desperately. *Not my father. Elowë, no.*

"There is no honor or praise I can give your father higher than what is being sung in Reachwind tonight," Silvanus somberly added. "Yet this wound has been the worst of all the Firewalkers have dealt. Here, I have lost my greatest friend, and from you, they have taken a father. Our only comfort is in knowing the glory he has entered at the Creator's side."

It can't be.

"Havarius."

Havarius looked through his tears at the mirror to meet the ones glistening on Silvanus' wrinkled cheeks.

"I… I should tell Mother," Havarius choked. He forced himself to stand upright and wiped his face with his palm.

"I spoke with Lina shortly after we returned. She and your sister know."

Havarius nodded, still trembling. "I don't know what to do. What do I do without him?"

Silvanus took a step away from the mirror, glancing towards the light of the setting sun. He turned back to Havarius, more resolved.

"I loved Orian and your family deeply, Havarius. The work we have done to protect Andaaya must continue. Will you join me in this?"

Havarius sucked in a breath, hardening his grief. "Yes. For him."

"Thank you, Havarius," he murmured. "Orian paid the ultimate price so that you and others might live. We shall not waste his sacrifice. And I believe our hope now lies with you. As I said, the Oathsworn are safe for the moment, but there are answers we must uncover before it is too late."

"Answers to what?"

"The Firewalkers' ultimate plan." Silvanus lightly tapped his staff. "Reachwind is not their true goal."

"Wait, what? But they nearly wiped out the core of our Order."

"The dragon notwithstanding, by only a token force and their prince," replied Silvanus. "The Firelord and the bulk of his Ilumancers were not present. Why forsake the glory? Why restrain himself from the destruction of our headquarters? By logic, it can only be some deeper plan is in motion we do not yet see."

"You think he's planning to strike somewhere else? Calharon?"

"Perhaps, but truthfully, I am unsure." Silvanus shrugged, leaning heavily on his staff. "Havarius, we are running out of time. I fear there is only one who holds the answers to our questions."

"Caelia."

"I am sorry. I know the difficulty this places upon you."

"And her."

Silvanus tilted his head. "Indeed, and the princess. But candidly, we are out of options. There is much I am willing to endure to save our people. Just as your father endured much. That is why I do not balk at your love or even your exposure to blood magic. The fate of the Oathsworn depends upon you. What say you, Havarius? What price are you willing to pay for our people?"

Havarius sighed and nodded.

Chapter 13
Truth

Havarius paced anxiously in the shadows of the hedge. Fear, hurt, and anger boiled inside him, contending for domination of his thoughts. He glanced towards the wall encircling the gardens, waiting for a glimpse of movement in the moonlight.

Why? he silently cried, scowling at the stars. *Why him? Creator, why did you let this happen?*

He collapsed onto the stone bench at the center, clenching his head in his hands. Tears threatened to begin anew as his breath quickened. He pounded the bench with a hand, gripping the edge with whitened knuckles.

"Havarius." He glanced up, a cry sticking in his throat. Caelia rushed over in her dark outfit, sliding next to him and wrapping him in her arms. "I know. Dragol told him. I'm so, so sorry, love."

Havarius shattered. Great sobs wracked his body, and only Caelia's gentle grasp kept him from tumbling into the dirt. Streams flowed from his eyes, wetting the edge of her clothing. She held him as he cried, overcome with despair. Only her love moored him in the whirlwind of pain overwhelming his soul. After what had felt an eternity, Havarius' cries slowed, weakened by grief.

"He—he's gone," Havarius choked. "He's gone. There's so much I didn't tell him. So much we didn't get to say…"

"I know. I am so sorry," she whispered, holding him tightly.

"Did you know about the dragon?" Havarius gasped, trying to tame his swirling misery.

"No," Caelia admitted. "Last I knew, my brother's voyage across the Far Sea involved some fabled blood mage shrine. I never expected…"

"That he'd return and kill my father?"

Caelia flinched, drawing back slightly. Havarius looked up at the hurt written across her face, tears forming.

"You are more my family than he is," she said, trembling. "You know I would have warned you. Do you really doubt me?"

Havarius sighed. "No, that was cruel. I'm sorry." She drew closer, lightly squeezing his hands.

"You're hurting, I understand. But I'm here for you. I love you. No matter what."

"I love you too."

For a moment, they were silent, staring at the surrounding leafy walls rustling in the faint nighttime breeze. Havarius drew in a breath and straightened, blinking slowly.

"I have to ask you something, for my father's sake."

She gripped his hands tighter. "Anything."

"Do you know what the Firelord is planning?"

Caelia paused, raising a slender brow. "What do you mean?"

"I… Look. Your father and his most powerful mages didn't attack Reachwind. The Oathsworn believe he's planning something, but have no idea what. We're running out of time, and now my mother and sister may be in danger. Silvanus hopes you might be able to help us protect them. He asked me—us—to spy on your father."

Caelia gasped. "*Havarius*! He knows about *us*?"

"He saw us after the peace summit earlier this year," he admitted. "But Cae, Silvanus knows and even welcomed it. He's kept our secret this whole time."

"Because he's using us," Caelia scoffed, folding her arms and scowling. "What happens when I betray my father and he gets what he wants? What happens to you?"

Havarius shrugged. "I trust him, Cae. He and my father were the closest of friends. He won't let anything happen to me, or you."

She studied him for several moments, still scowling. Doubt began to creep into Havarius' mind. Had he made the wrong choice? Had he pushed her too far?

Finally, Caelia sighed, glaring suspicion exchanged for weary resignation. "We knew revealing our love meant one or both of our peoples would banish us. Honestly, it's always seemed like we had a better chance with the Oathsworn, anyway. Ever since I came to Nalindor—really since Mother died—my father hasn't been the same. He's cold, distant. Like I'm failing him at every turn while my brother is a prodigy. And I'm, I'm either not wanted or not doing what's expected or..." Her voice trailed off and she bit her lip, tears forming.

Havarius scooted closer, hugging her close and turning her face towards his. "You are perfect and beautiful and strong. You move with this incredible grace and confidence, greater than any of the Elvish lords. It's inspiring to see you lead and serve those around you. You are worth more than anything, Caelia. And somehow, I'm just lucky enough to love you."

He saw her doubt vanish, replaced with loving adoration as she held his gaze. She cuddled into his arms, holding tightly and resting her head against his.

"Thank you," she murmured. "I love you, Havarius."

"I love you too."

He pressed his lips against hers, a long, gentle kiss, losing himself in their love.

Caelia sighed as she pulled back, her gleaming eyes fixed on him. "I want to help you and Silvanus, but I don't know what my father is planning. He's very secretive—at least with me. Most of his war councils don't involve me. I couldn't even get a straight answer from him about what happened in the Halls."

Havarius nodded, thinking. "But he trusts you enough to lead the embassy in Nalindor."

Caelia gave a short laugh. "It's a token position because I'm Firewalker royalty. My father couldn't care less about the Elves and their traditions. He'll make appearances for King Fael's summons and things like Dragon Day to placate him and keep the Elves out of the war. But really, the embassy functions more as a rest stop for my father's messengers between the front and Sabron. And, you know, 'rapport building' for recruitment."

Havarius perked up. "Messengers?"

"Usually, intelligence passing between him and commanders like Dragol that he doesn't want to share through the iluvimír. He's still paranoid there are more mirrors out there that can spy on ours. I don't have the authority to review any messages without his permission, though."

"I'm guessing I don't either," Havarius teased. "Wouldn't be the first time I took something without permission."

Caelia's eyes widened. "Wait. You want to break into the embassy?"

Havarius grinned. "I happen to know someone who knows all the guard rotations and where keys are kept."

Caelia shook her head, stifling a smile. "You're crazy. You realize what will happen if they catch you? If they catch *us*?"

"Um, we don't have to wait for Dragon Day to tell your father?"

She laughed. "Fair point."

"Come on, Cae. This could be our only chance. I have to do something. I can't let my father's death mean nothing." Caelia's playfulness faded into a gentle smile.

"I understand," she murmured. "Your father was always brave and kind, even to me after every exchange with my father. I think that's part of why I liked you so much. I could always see how you reflected the best parts of him."

Tears threatened to rain once more as Havarius choked down a sob. He squeezed her delicate hand, closing his eyes as he rested his head against hers. Caelia straightened, taking a deep breath as Havarius looked at her.

She nodded. "Let's go."

Chapter 14
Secrets of the Flame

Thick clouds blanketed the midnight sky over desolate streets. Faint lamplight glistened in the fog, reflecting off the white stone tower at the end of the thoroughfare that led to the looming walls of the Firewalker embassy. Beyond its iron gates, a soldier in dark armor leaned listlessly on his polished spear before the massive carved doors of the estate. Flameless arcane orbs pulsed lazily on either side of the entry, casting shadows into the street. The manor rose several stories, the steep curve of its roof towering over the surrounding district and trees, save a few hennaleth that rivaled its height.

Havarius padded after Caelia as she slipped between a row of houses near the walls, their windows like black voids peering into the empty lane. She stopped at the edge, pressing against the cold stone veiled in the gloom. Havarius slid beside her, leaning close and holding his breath.

"There's a spot where the road narrows on the far side," Caelia mumbled into his ear. "Have your magic ready for the jump. Once we're in the courtyard, don't stop. There's an open window on the second floor, west side. I was planning to come back that way, anyway."

"You always slip out like this?" Havarius whispered with a grin.

Caelia shrugged. "My father is very particular about everyone's schedules, mine included. Besides, I seem to recall someone else's penchant for rooftop strolls." She glanced towards the guard, who shifted and stretched. "The watchmen will switch in a minute. This way."

She dashed from the shadows, angling away from the embassy gates towards the far corner where a large oak stretched beyond the impenetrable wall. Havarius sprinted after her as quietly as he could, hardly able to track her dark figure in the deepness of the night. She reached the corner and raced on, passing the first building and swerving around it. Havarius followed on her heels. As Caelia bounded up a flight of stairs to a patio overlooking a small market square, Havarius sensed her magic waxing. He pressed into the Current, feeling a shock of energy flood his limbs.

Caelia threw out her arm, stopping him. "Wait for it... Now!"

She launched across the narrow lane with inhuman force, skipping lightly off the embassy's wall, and vanished silently into the swaying oak leaves. Havarius sucked in his breath and leapt. His stomach dropped as his feet left the ground, excitement and thrill coursing. He landed on the masonry, wobbling, then jumped awkwardly towards a massive limb running parallel to the wall. He clutched the trunk to steady himself, glancing towards the courtyard beyond. No sign of the guards.

Cautiously, he lowered himself onto the grassy earth, spotting Caelia sprinting closer to the estate's darkened exterior as he cleared the growth. He raced after her, letting the magic carry him with increased speed.

Caelia angled towards a corner of the building hidden from the courtyard, where a wing extended to the west. Havarius spotted the open window, the silhouette of curtains billowing faintly in the dark. She ran straight to the opposing wall, launching herself into the air with an unnatural height. She flexed against the stone, springing back towards the window ledge where she swung over the sill and was gone. Havarius fixed onto the same spot, summoning another burst of magic to carry him into the air. His boots slipped against the cool bricks and he gasped, leaping at the ledge with outstretched arms. He clutched the edge, dangling for a moment, before flailing his way up. Suddenly Caelia appeared, grabbing his arms and tugging him into the lightless room. Havarius collapsed, pulling her down with him as he gasped for air.

"Thanks," he wheezed, rolling to the side.

"Looks like you could use some practice," she teased in a whisper as she staggered to her feet. She pulled the loose strands of her hair out of her face and straightened her tunic.

"Let's not make a habit of it," Havarius grunted, clambering from the floor. "Where are we?"

"A guest room not far from mine." She crept to a strip of light gleaming near the floor. As his eyes adjusted, Havarius could make out the posters of a wide, luxurious bed and pieces of carved furniture along the walls. Inscrutable paintings and banners covered the walls, shrouded in black. More light sprang into the room as Caelia teased the door open, peeking into the hall.

"My father's study is on the first floor, opposite side from here. That'll be our best bet," she explained. "The guards at the central stairs will change in five minutes. We'll make our move for the east stairwell, and then the dash for the room as the night man wraps up below and heads this way."

"And getting out?"

"Retrace our steps, or there's another oak on the south lawn to make for," Caelia whispered. "And either way, pray that Elowë hides us." She glanced once more into the hall. "Ready?" Havarius nodded.

Caelia's dark figure slipped into the light, followed closely by Havarius. They crept through the high-ceilinged hall, following the train of crimson carpet as it turned back towards the main building. Great iron chandeliers bathed the stone walls in pulsating light, preventing any hope of secrecy. Dusky banners emblazoned with the Firewalker seal, a narrow, golden sword wrapped in red flames, lined the corridor. Havarius scanned each door they passed, half expecting one of them to fling open and unleash a swarm of Firewalkers.

Caelia halted at the next turn, crouching low, and signaled for Havarius to stop. She pressed against the rough blocks, peeking at the lofty stairwell beyond. After a few moments, heavy boots echoed loudly down the bare steps. As the sound retreated, Caelia waved her hand and darted into the hall. They stole towards the far end as fast as they dared, praying the plush rug would dampen the noise. Without stopping, Caelia swerved around the far corner and out of sight. After another series of turns with more sealed doors and brightly lit halls, they came to a rounded staircase bathed in gloom, save a faint light from an occasional window facing the embassy grounds. They warily descended to the lower floor, hugging the central pillar.

As the light from the hall grew, Caelia slowed their pace, inching forwards for a glimpse. After a moment, she slipped onto the soft flooring of the passage and Havarius followed. The first floor resembled the other, save slightly lower ceilings, which gave the chandeliers a more ominous tone, as if they waited eagerly to reveal the intruders. A handful of paces forward, the hall split and Caelia led them left, away from the manor's entrance. After passing two more doors, she paused, listening against the solid wood of another. With a final glance around the hall, she gripped the iron handle, gently releasing the latch. She teased it open just enough for the pair to slip through, before quickly sealing it shut.

Darkness enveloped Havarius once more, and he stumbled in blindness. He was aware that Caelia had left his side, creeping towards the far wall. The faint scuffle of hinges opening and small objects being moved aside reached him, amplified in the desolate void. A sharp twinge bit into Havarius' hip as he collided with some solid piece of furniture and he grunted. Suddenly, the room burst with light as Caelia summoned a spark of flame, breathing life into a thin candle atop the silver holder in her hand.

Havarius surveyed the study, marveling at how similar it was to his father's. There were fewer books and more displays—old swords, ancient relics, and strange metallic sculptures—but even a wide mahogany desk dominated the far end. More Firewalker banners hung from the gloomy walls between the cases.

Caelia slid around the desk, focused on something behind the large, ornate chair. Havarius moved closer as she fiddled with the engraved sliding door of a low cabinet lining the back wall. She undid the latch and pushed back the screen, revealing a wide, steel safe hidden within. She pulled a small key from the pocket of her leggings, inserted it into the slot, and turned. The safe released a muted click. As Caelia swung open the safe, Havarius saw rows upon rows of little scrolls, organized by metal dividers. Caelia ran her slender finger along the bottom, pausing beside the tiny labels of each section. She plucked one from the middle with a satisfied hum and brought it to the desk. Havarius watched her expectantly.

"Do you know what we're looking for?" he whispered, drawing close.

"Not exactly. The missives are organized by region and date: who they're going to and when. Ones directly involving my father are probably our best hope."

"You don't review these often, then?"

"No. Like I said, only when he approves it, which generally is when I'm standing here waiting for him to finish reading one."

Havarius walked back towards the safe as she skimmed the first letter. He perused the collection of labels, studying the names of locations around Andaaya. He noticed the ones on the left and deeper in the safe appeared older. Beside the hinges there was a narrower section, unmarked. Only a couple of scrolls occupied the bay. Curious, Havarius pulled one out and rejoined Caelia. He unfurled the dry parchment, holding it flat on the smooth wood. He took one look at the paper and gasped.

"What?" Caelia breathed, nearly jumping out of her boots.

"The Halls," Havarius answered. He moved the missive into the light. "It's to Firelord Turgaen from a Captain Marlond. 'Report on the Liberation of the Halls of Eternal Slumber'."

"Well? What does it say?"

Havarius hurriedly scanned the document. "His company was responsible for invading the Halls during the sack of Autumnhold. It says he confirmed no survivors, as ordered. Left behind Oathsworn evidence, again, as ordered. And... hmm, that's odd."

"What?"

Havarius glanced at her, confused. "All iluvasil, the captain says, 'confirmed transported to rendezvous. Awaiting phase two.'"

"My father has never spoken of iluvasil," Caelia said seriously.

"The only shards I know of are the ones from the Halls and those the Elves keep at the palace for the Joining."

"And phase two of what, I wonder?"

Havarius shrugged. "Maybe whatever plan Silvanus is searching for."

Caelia hurried back to the safe, scanning the contents. Havarius watched as she hunched beside it, eyes darting.

"What are you looking for?"

"Marlond. He sounds familiar. Anything here that might be directed to... Ah!" Caelia gripped a set of scrolls, tossing them onto the desk. She peeled open the first, her bright hair quivering as she eagerly scanned the message.

"That's why," she muttered. "A *Commander* Marlond was recently assigned to Nalindor from Dor Telmon. Seems he was promoted. I thought it strange such a ranking officer was coming."

"Is he here?"

"It's likely by now, but I haven't met or heard from him. There's a barracks near the southern gate where most of the soldiers rotating through the area stay. He could be there, though it would be odd for a leading officer. They almost always claim a room here in the embassy."

Caelia grabbed a second scroll tied with a neat, silken ribbon and sealed with the Firewalker emblem. She looked at Havarius, then carefully pried off the wax and unfurled the scroll. After a moment of reading, her brilliant eyes grew wide. Havarius raised a brow and leaned closer.

"Father, how could you?" she gasped. Her whole body trembled as she lifted the letter, rereading it.

"Caelia?"

She turned to Havarius, tears forming. "Dragon Day. It's a trap. Not just for the Oathsworn, but the Elves, too. He's going to kill them all."

"*What*?" Havarius gripped the back of the massive chair. "What do you mean?"

"Phase two," she read, shivering, "of 'the Glorious Victory and the Flame Eternal'. Commander Marlond has been infiltrating Nalindor, using the refugee camp as a cover. My father's Ilumancers are spread across the city *right now*, posing as war refugees and ready with the iluvasil from the Halls. They're waiting for his signal to launch a final assault, toppling not just the Oathsworn but the Elvish council along with them."

"Every commander and delegate across Andaaya will be here for the final ceremony," Havarius groaned. "With that much power, they'll literally be unstoppable."

"The streets will be packed with festivalgoers," Caelia breathed, gripping his arm. "Havarius, it will be a bloodbath. We have to stop him. We have to warn the high king."

"And Silvanus. Will King Fael believe us though? He wasn't keen on believing the Oathsworn last time."

"But now we have evidence signed by my father himself, and... And you have me."

Havarius' eyes widened as he faced her. "You can't come back here if you do this. He'll banish you once he finds out."

"I think banishment is the least he will do," she muttered and bit her lip, glancing down. "The palace is the only place I'll be safe."

Havarius kissed her lightly on the forehead, hugging her close. "I won't let anything happen to you, Cae. We should go."

Caelia looked up, relief mixing with fear. She nodded, stuffing the scroll into her pocket, and then shoved the other scrolls back into the safe. Havarius moved over to the door as she snuffed out the candle and joined him. Caelia cracked open the door and peered into the hall. Then she slipped from the shadows in the direction they had first come. Just as Havarius was about to step from the dark, the clank of heavy boots rang off the stone floor. Caelia gasped and Havarius staggered back, pressing himself against the clammy blocks.

"Princess?" said a man's gruff voice, laced with confusion. "Sorry to startle you, my lady. I hadn't expected to find you down here."

"Oh no, it's quite alright," Caelia hurriedly replied. "I, I couldn't sleep and thought a walk might calm my mind."

"Yes, my lady," said the soldier hesitantly. "Well, since you are awake, I should inform you we received word moments ago from the barracks to prepare quarters for a distinguished officer without delay."

"Oh?" said Caelia, trying to sound casual.

"Yes, princess. Commander Marlond of the Dor Telmon garrison is arriving any moment for an extended stay, as Firelord Turgaen's personal guest. Actually, we could use your assistance in selecting the proper chambers. Could I trouble you, Princess Caelia?"

"Of course."

Havarius' heart raced. *What are you doing?*

"Thank you, my lady."

Caelia's soft footfalls faded as she moved away from the door.

"I believe there is a suitable room not far from mine," she said loudly. "It will have a much better view than one facing the *south lawn.*"

"As you say, princess."

Havarius risked a look around the doorframe, spotting Caelia's flowing hair as she rounded the corner. She glanced back, their eyes locking. She nodded briefly towards the hall, then vanished.

Blood pounded in Havarius' ears and the room spun. He clutched the edge of the frame, steadying himself.

Please no, he silently cried. *Elowë, what in Aldaria do I do now?*

Silvanus. He would know.

Havarius scanned the quiet corridor once more. Nothing.

Cautiously, he stepped into the light and paused, glancing at the spot where Caelia had disappeared. Then he turned, speeding down the long hall as silently as he could. He could hardly breathe, hardly think.

The oak. Find the oak.

After another turn, Havarius came to a doorway opening to a large, dimly lit sitting room. Rather than enter, he opened the door on his left, shuffling into a dark storeroom filled with an odd assortment of tightly organized wardrobes, chairs, and stacked chests. Faint moonlight fell through a small window on the far end, and through it, Havarius could see the high walls of the embassy grounds. He moved closer, prying loose the window latch and slowly inching it open. Across the lawn of low shrubs, manicured trees, and gravel paths, he spotted a massive, gnarled oak slightly to his left. Havarius gave a sigh of relief, and guilt instantly flooded him. Yet he knew there was no way he could rescue Caelia without exposing everything.

Please protect her, he prayed. *Give her another way.*

Havarius lowered himself from the ledge, crouching low as he raced along a row of thick evergreen shrubs lining a path straight towards the oak. So far, he couldn't see any Firewalkers patrolling this side. As he neared the end of the shrubs still several paces from the oak, he stopped and looked over the growth. A light bobbed into view, rounding the far side of the embassy. A soldier strolled aimlessly along the path, his flickering torch casting shadows across the walls.

With not a second to lose, Havarius summoned a burst of magic and sped across the open grass, leaping onto the lowest branches of the tree. He clambered higher into the thick foliage until he was certain he was hidden from view, then looked back. The soldier continued to stroll around the perimeter of the garden, making his way closer. Havarius climbed until he was level with the embassy wall, shimmying across a branch stretching beside the stone. With a final spurt of magic, he leapt, bursting from the leaves and over the wall. He grabbed the edge as he sailed over, bashing against the outside and ignoring the pain, before dropping to the street. He landed hard and rolled, grunting. Then he stood and dusted his legs, taking a final wistful glance at the wall that withheld his heart.

Havarius sighed and turned, vanishing among the shadows.

Chapter 15
Betrayed

Caelia's heart pounded as she led the soldier into the manor entry, praying the man hadn't noticed her edginess. She quickened her stride, the jingling of the man's armor increasing as she ushered him further from Havarius. The groggy eyes of the guards in the lofty foyer drifted towards them before the men straightened and gripped their halberds more firmly. She breezed past them without a second glance, mounting the wide stairwell to the upper floor. Even now, the warm lights of the halls seemed to relish her fear, as if at any moment they could expose her.

Caelia turned left, heading back down the passage where she and Havarius had begun. Although she was loath to offer it, she knew which room an officer of Marlond's rank would likely expect. She paused outside the carved door, her fingers resting on the cool metal of the handle.

How would she escape now? Could she make it to the south lawn before Commander Marlond arrived? What if another sentry discovered her along the way? For a terrible moment, all

Caelia could see was Havarius, cornered by Firewalkers against the manor wall, their weapons gleaming in the blaze of flames around him. Death waiting to spring. She shuddered.

"My lady?" said the soldier, jolting Caelia back to reality. She shook the image from her head.

"Have the steward bring lights for the room and ensure the commander's attendants know where to bring his belongings," Caelia directed, pushing open the door. She stepped into the shadows, feeling the cool, moist breeze of the open window swirl around her. She stepped to the opening, pausing once more to look across the lawn at the tree she and Havarius had entered from, veiled in shadows. Caelia pulled the window shut with a swift motion.

"Yes, princess," replied the soldier with a salute before his heavy boots thumped away.

She left the room, striding quickly towards her own. Once inside, she summoned a flame to light the candle beside the bed, then hastily changed into a more formal amber gown. She pulled the little scroll from her father's office from her discarded leggings and shoved it in the nightstand drawer. Now was not the time to disappear. For all she knew, Havarius was still waiting for his chance to escape. She needed to buy him time. She allowed her nerves to overpower the growing fatigue, no longer sure even what hour of the night it was.

Caelia returned to the hall, passing the aging steward as he shambled into the guest room with his bundle of supplies. The murmur of voices and rattle of objects drifted from the grand stairwell. A tickle of fear-laced doubt rose in her chest. She had already committed to betraying her father, betraying everything she had ever known. Could she bear the masquerade before one of her father's highest officers?

I must, she told herself. *Elowë, protect me.*

With a heavy step, she marched into the foyer.

A mass of soldiers and porters scurried about the floor below as Caelia turned and descended the landing. Several looked up to see her, redoubling their focus as guards formed rows beside the entry walls and baggage handlers scampered out of the way. Caelia stopped near the end of the guards, smoothing the wrinkles from her dress as the clamor subsided. From the gloom beyond the lamps of the great entry, a tall figure emerged, the gold etchings in his ebony armor catching the light as he moved. The commander's chestnut hair and beard came into view, dark eyes quickly spotting Caelia, where she waited with a warm expression to conceal the inner turmoil. He crossed the foyer, his metallic boots clicking against the smooth stone, his gaze never leaving her. He stopped, bowing slightly before her, and the soldiers raised their arms in salute. The commander rose with a confident smile.

"Princess Caelia," Marlond began. "I did not expect your welcome at such an hour. I implore your pardon."

Caelia dipped her head. "Welcome to Nalindor, Commander Marlond. We are honored to receive you. There is no fault of yours, only the happy chance that I should be available to greet our guests. I trust your journey from Dor Telmon was quiet?"

"Indeed. And I am most looking forward to inspecting our attachment here in Nalindor."

"Oh?" Fear tingled up her spine.

"Did your father not send word?" said Marlond, raising a brow. "No doubt there are more pressing matters on his mind. I am to ensure the embassy and its personnel are made presentable for his arrival before the festival is upon us."

"My father is coming? For Dragon Day?" she asked, feigning ignorance.

Marlond gave a short chuckle. "Why, of course, princess. Surely you expect, just as I, that the Firelord would not miss such a *momentous* occasion?" The way he lingered over the word made her skin crawl.

"No, I suppose he wouldn't," she almost whispered, glancing away. Marlond watched her, the curiosity in his gaze growing. Caelia snapped her attention back. "Our embassy is open to you, commander. I am happy to assist, however I may."

Marlond nodded. "Thank you, princess. I will endeavor not to disturb your other duties as much as possible. Still, there is much to do."

"Yes," agreed Caelia, "though even soldiers must rest. I expect you and your men are weary. I have ordered the officers' chamber opened for your arrival. Allow me to show to your quarters."

Marlond bowed again, hesitating as she turned. "I am most grateful. Though, there is a matter I must see to first. The steward I'm sure will—"

"My dear commander," Caelia interrupted with a light laugh, spinning back to him. "We are only a few hours from dawn's light. Surely it can wait for fresher eyes." She gestured towards the stairs as Marlond's stare hardened. "Your rest here will no doubt chase away all exhaustion from the road, leaving you refreshed for the toil ahead. This way, if you please."

For a moment she feared she'd overstepped, dooming herself and all their plans. Commander Marlond let out a small sigh.

"As you say, princess."

Caelia's trembling hand found the banister as she stepped forward, not daring to glance back at the boots stomping after her. They marched to the commander's room in silence, her nerves overpowering any sense of awkwardness in the in between. At the door, Caelia curtsied before gesturing to the now warmly lit chamber. Marlond bowed stiffly.

"I thank you, princess, for your hospitality," he said cooly. "I look forward to our preparations."

"Indeed," she replied, keeping her voice level. "Rest well, commander."

She turned, heading to her own door, still feeling the man's stare boring into her as she slipped inside. Her heart threatened to burst from her chest as she slumped against the door, scanning the room to make sure it was empty. Her escape tonight now seemed impossible. The window to the courtyard was completely out of the question, and likely any attempt to sneak past Marlond to the south lawn would raise his suspicions. Caelia ran her fingers through a tangled strand of hair, moving towards the bed. There was nothing she could do now, save pray that morning brought a new chance.

Her fingers trembled as she fumbled with her dress and slipped into her nightgown, exhaustion overtaking her. She climbed into the soft comfort of the bed, staring at the nightstand beneath the flickering candle, and the horrible secret it concealed. She turned onto her back, staring at the shadows on the ceiling.

"Elowë," she whispered, "protect Havarius. Save me."

She reached over and softly blew out the light.

⸺◆⸺

The warm sun streamed through the open curtains of the window as Caelia groaned, rubbing the soreness from her eyes as she sat up. She opened them wider. How long had she slept? *It must be nearly mid-morning!*

She leapt out of bed, hurriedly changing and fixing her hair before a long rectangular mirror in the corner. Caelia strode towards the door, yanking it open. She gasped, nearly tripping as she stepped back. "Commander!"

Commander Marlond bowed gracefully, wearing the same smile above his impeccable armor from the night before. "Princess Caelia. My apologies for startling you. I was just about to knock."

"It's quite alright," Caelia replied, composing herself. "How may I help you? I trust you slept well?"

"Quite well. Actually, there is a rather urgent situation in the reception hall that requires your expertise. I came to fetch you immediately."

Caelia raised her brows, stepping closer. "Of course. Please, commander, lead on."

Anxiety returned like an unwelcomed friend as she chased after Marlond. On the main floor, he led her through the foyer, down a short side hall, and opened the door to a wide, high-ceilinged room overlooking the cheery green of the front lawn. A collection of leather chairs and sofas dotted the room, beams from the morning sun filling the chamber and lightening the furniture's dark tone. An older man awkwardly shifted from leg to leg between one seat and the high windows. As Marlond's weighty boots clicked against the stone, the man's graying hair and wrinkled face swerved to meet them. He straightened his fraying tunic as he bowed low.

"Arn?" said Caelia, confused. The leading representative of the refugee camp had never come himself to the Firewalker embassy.

"My lady," Arn rasped, bowing again. "I hope I'm not intruding, but I wasn't sure what else to do."

Caelia glanced at Marlond. "Of course not. You are most welcome. How can I help you?"

The old man's gaze flicked towards the commander hesitantly. "It, it's about the camp, my lady. The caravan that was to arrive with the next shipment of supplies."

"Yes, the one from Sabron. What news of it?"

"It didn't make it, princess. Some of the soldiers found it, raided by bandits they said it was."

The color drained from Caelia's face. "That, that's not possible. The route was secured. I had a full assurance from the garrison in Sabron. There were weeks of food and medical supplies in those carts!"

Marlond cleared his throat. "If I may, princess. It was a detachment of my men who found the remains. They brought word back to Nalindor as quickly as they could."

"Princess Caelia," said Arn, faintly trembling, "you know as I do how desperately we needed that shipment. Food is low and the new survivors from Autumnhold took up most of the remaining bandages and salves. The supplies in camp won't last the week unless we do something."

"I know," Caelia murmured, biting her lip. "I need a moment to think. There must be another way."

"I requested the details of other merchants the Order has operating between Nalindor and our larger cities," Marlond offered, gesturing to a stack of papers atop a wide table beside the paneled wall. "Perhaps something in these will assist you."

"Yes, thank you, commander." Caelia nodded gratefully.

"I'm afraid I must excuse myself for the moment," the commander continued. "I have other duties to attend to this morning."

"Of course. Thank you for bringing this to my attention, Commander Marlond." Caelia curtsied as Marlond saluted and left the room. She turned back to Arn, his weary eyes shifting between her and the table. "Arn, do you have time to look through these with me? You may know some of these merchants if they have traveled through Nalindor recently."

"I'd be happy to, my lady."

For the next hour or so, Caelia and Arn pored over the stack of schedules and routes, hoping for some alternative they could quickly arrange. No clear answer though came to them. There was simply too much required for any one of the nearby vendors to fulfill before things became dire. Caelia stood back from the table, frowning deeply.

"I'm afraid we must do what is most uncomfortable," she said after several moments of silence. Arn nodded resignedly. "See that the other leaders begin the rationing immediately. I will send missives to the handful of these merchants who are closest in the hopes of getting the most pressing supplies delivered soon, remedying the food situation first."

"Yes, my lady." Arn bowed and hurried from the room.

Caelia lingered a while longer, praying for some detail they had overlooked, to no avail. The chaos of the war with the Oathsworn had only made things more difficult, especially as the ferocity increased. There were simply too few she could call on now, and despair threatened to consume her. She shook her head, taking a deep breath as her fingers dug into the polished wood of the table. These people were her responsibility. They depended on her to lead. Even if she was about to abandon it all. Maybe she could at least see this through.

"There has to be a way," she whispered.

At last, Caelia stepped away from the table, her hunger gnawing as she glanced out at the embassy grounds. It had to be nearly midday now. She felt a pang of guilt as she stepped towards the door, making a mental note to ask the steward about the embassy's own reserves before drafting the merchant letters in her head as she reached for the handle.

"Oh! Commander Marlond," she breathed, nearly tripping to keep from crashing into him. His towering figure stood inches from the door with a frown, his black and gold gauntlets folded over his chest. "We ought to stop meeting like this."

Marlond's expression didn't change. "Indeed."

A tenseness filled the momentary silence.

"Arn has left for the refugee camp," said Caelia. "Is... there something you need from me?"

"Walk with me, princess." He gestured for her to join him in the passage, and she stepped hesitantly forward.

"I was actually heading for the dining hall, commander. Would you care to join me?"

"This way, please." Marlond's boots clattered as he turned away from the hall to the foyer and down another passage. Caelia paused.

"Can this wait, commander? I feel rather faint at the moment."

He wheeled around to her, his dark eyes gleaming. "No, it cannot."

A roll of parchment appeared from his side, crinkling in his armored grip. Caelia's heart stopped.

The scroll.

"I, I am not sure I understand," she stammered. How could she have been so stupid to forget it?

"Understand what, princess?" Marlond said in a low, savage tone. "How a private correspondence from the Firelord ended up in your nightstand? Considering who holds the keys, I can fathom a guess."

Caelia sucked in a breath, clenching her fist. "You have no right to accuse me, commander. Do not forget where your loyalty lies."

"Nor yours," he growled. He stepped closer, looming over her. Caelia moved to raise her fist, pulling from the Current. Marlond snatched her hand, roughly dragging her off balance as his presence barreled against her consciousness, forcing her to retreat. "Don't try it."

She twisted in his steely grip, pain radiating as he squeezed tighter. "Let me go!"

Marlond tugged her forward, spinning back towards the outer hall. "This way, *princess*."

Caelia stumbled after him, only the echo of his boots piercing the silence. They were heading for the storerooms and cellar, away from the wings where most of the staff and guards would be. With a sinking dread, she knew where Marlond was taking her, even if she had never set foot there herself.

"Release me, at once!"

Marlond forced her on, not even pausing as she slipped down the damp stairs into the blackness of the manor basement. He summoned a small flame above his palm, the flicker casting threatening shadows in the veiled doorways and clutter lining the nearly abandoned passage. He turned aside, shoving open a barred iron door with a horrendous creak. With a motion as quick as lightning, Marlond flicked a pair of fingers towards the ceiling. The dust and web-streaked flameless orbs of the room's iron chandelier gasped to life. He dragged her forward, releasing his grip as Caelia staggered into the room. She spun around, fear, shame, and fury behind her flashing eyes.

"How dare you," she hissed.

Marlond's cold glare didn't even balk as he paused beside the door. "You will wait here until I return. Don't try anything foolish. You know as well as I do the consequences." He slammed the door, the metal screeching as the bar fell into place. Marlond's muffled boots faded down the tunnel, leaving only the dreary emptiness of the shadowed cell.

Caelia spun around, taking in the dank blocks of the walls. She took a step closer to the bed's iron frame in the corner, shivering as the floor rattled under her shoes. She glanced down, noticing the reflective surface in the light. Somewhere behind the walls, she knew there was a device tuned to the Current of the room. Any change to the room's energy, and the iluvan would shock the floor, and anything inside. Caelia shuddered again. What sort of barbarism had her father's predecessors undertaken here, under the very noses of the Elves? What sort had *he*?

Caelia collapsed onto the stiff sheets, her stomach growling as she stared up at the featureless rock. Instead of despair or sorrow, she found anger rising. Anger at Marlond and her father, yes, but also herself. How had she not seen the depth of her father's depravity until now? Why had she waited so long, tried so hard to appease him? Just because she was his daughter? She scowled in the dark. He'd never treated her like one. Not in all the years of her adulthood, at the very least. And now, would he see her as his daughter, or another threat to his reign?

Caelia turned onto her side, sighing. She feared she knew.

Chapter 16
Stones of Fate

Silvanus stared blankly at the rolling forest, a gentle breeze wafting across the grand porch of the Keep. The sun's first rays pierced the clouds racing overhead as dawn gathered its strength. The sweet melody of a songbird echoed from the trees of the courtyard. Yet still, it all seemed bitter to him. The mountains to the south bore into him like ravenous specters, daring him to gaze upon that cursed peak once more. He was not worthy of such blessings when so many others would rise to see the dawn no more. Silvanus closed his eyes, pulling in a breath.

"Grandmaster, sir," a small voice peeped from the wide entryway. Silvanus slowly turned, running a hand through his shaggy, white hair.

"Good morning, Lieutenant Jorin," he greeted wearily. He shook away the despairing thoughts. There was much still to do.

"Sir, Captain Heran requests a moment of your time, if you would meet him in the lower hall."

"Yes, of course." Silvanus nodded. "Thank you, Jorin."

The soldier bowed, his light mail clinking as he rose and marched back into the gloomy corridor. Temptation finally overcame Silvanus, and he glanced at the snowy peak, reduced to an oddly flat plane among the others. He shuddered, averting his eyes. Then he shuffled into the Keep, his staff gently clicking against the stone.

Silvanus followed the maze of lofty halls, glass orbs of golden light guiding the way as occasional shafts from the sun spilled through open doors. After several turns, he descended a stairwell leading deeper into the heart of Reachwind Keep. The rough walls grew cold and clammy, the low ceiling pressing in as orbs grew sparser and the shadows longer. Another long passage ended at a simple wooden door. Silvanus pushed it open, feeling refreshed as cleaner air rushed over him.

The large chamber was well lit. Grand chandeliers of more arcane lights hung from the slab high above. Rows of thick wooden shelving lined the far wall, and several tall bookcases crammed with papers and tomes flanked the one on his right. Beyond a row of tables and benches to his left, mages in gray and blue robes and several soldiers in mail and leather armor scurried about in a sea of wooden crates. Stacks of books, vials of colored liquid, and an array of metallic instruments were being organized into groups, hastily loaded into the containers and sealed. Captain Heran stood from the center of chaos, hurrying over once he spotted Silvanus.

"Grandmaster Silvanus, thank you for coming," he huffed, wiping sweat from his brow.

Silvanus smiled faintly. "Are we on schedule?"

"Yes, sir. Most of these will be shipped within the hour. The wagons are being prepared as we speak."

"Very good. And the relic?"

Heran motioned for Silvanus to follow as he led past the thick of the activity and towards the far corner. The smoky glass of the white polished obelisk shifted in the light as they approached. A faint blue glow emanated from the small glass case near the front of its base, and Silvanus could feel the power thrumming inside. Yet not quite as strong as it had been in the Halls.

"We haven't completed our research," Heran explained, moving beside the pod. "We need more time to finish the prototype and perform the tests. But I promise it won't be long before the shield is ready."

"I am afraid time is not on our side," said Silvanus. "Firewalkers have been spotted at the foot of the pass. They are melting through the avalanche. The project must be continued elsewhere."

"Sir?"

"You are to join our contact in Ostinlaë. We cannot risk the Firewalkers discovering our intention. Sanctuary among the Elves will provide some measure of security. Plus, our Elvish friend's knowledge may hasten our progress. Should the Keep fall, this iluvashtin may be Calharon's last hope."

Heran bowed. "As you say, sir. I will have a summary of our progress sent to your quarters."

Silvanus nodded and studied the pod a moment more in brooding silence.

Heran took a step forward before he added in a low voice, "What of the other item?"

"Is it prepared?"

Heran reached into a leather pouch strapped to the belt over his silver mail. He pulled out his fist, a subtle, white light twinkling through his fingers. He turned, keeping his back to the others as Silvanus' eyes gleamed. Heran opened his hand.

A small ring of polished silver rested in his palm, delicate lines and leaflike patterns woven across the band. But most captivating was the stone. A perfect oval of pure white crystal adorned the setting, light swirling under its shell. Silvanus brushed the shard with his mind, feeling its ocean of power ripple through the Current.

"As you described, sir," Heran murmured, stretching out his hand. Silvanus carefully took the ring, marveling at it from every angle.

"Your craftsman is most skilled. Very well done, my friend."

"The iluvashtin has also been reinforced with additional iluvan," Heran added. "It should be more than enough to compensate. Though, if I may, sir, I still do not understand the relationship between the pod and the iluvasil."

"The ring is needed for another matter," Silvanus quickly answered. "Its part in our efforts here is complete."

"Yes, grandmaster."

Silvanus slipped the ring into the pocket of his robe. "Thank you, Heran. Please proceed with the rest. Our contact in Ostinlaë is expecting you."

"Yes, sir." Heran bowed once more, then joined the others sorting through the crates.

Two of the soldiers drew near to Silvanus, still lost in thought. He watched as they cast a long linen cloth over the iluvashtin, drawing it tight against the base.

Elowë, let it be enough, he silently prayed.

Silvanus turned, passing through the crates and their hurried caretakers, and slipped back into the hall without another word.

Silvanus sat at the modest desk near the window of his quarters, studying the leather-bound journal from Heran's scribe. There were many gaps still to fill in their logic, still so much mere mortals had yet to comprehend of the elder race. Yet there was hope. If Reachwind could withstand the wrath of the Firewalkers, perhaps this desperate attempt would bear fruit from the ashes he had trod in the Halls all those moons ago. Silvanus dared to hold that hope.

And yet... He pulled the iluvasil ring from his side, rolling it in his fingers.

What trick shall we play? Orian's voice echoed in his head. His heart ached.

A sudden knock startled him from his thoughts.

"Enter," he called, concealing it. As he rose from the worn chair and grasped his staff, a girl in thin, leathered armor and hardly of adult age rushed into the room, bowing low. She shoved loose strands of black hair behind her ears, rising nervously.

"Grandmaster Silvanus," she breathed. "A message for you, from Ambassador Stormcrown."

Silvanus arched his brows. "Havarius?"

"Yes, grandmaster. The iluvimír is ready. He says it's urgent."

He nodded. "Thank you. I shall be there momentarily."

The girl bowed and darted from the room. Silvanus glanced at the journal, then closed the cover and sighed. He straightened the edge of his soft, ashen tunic and stepped into the wide hall. After several turns and descending a wide flight of stairs, Silvanus opened the heavy door to the small, lofty chamber. Daylight lit the rocky walls through the towering bank of windows, brightening the deep blue and silver rug spanning the room. Across from him, the large iluvimír shimmered, an image of the Oathsworn embassy's study glowing in the center of its azure depths. Havarius paced rapidly in and out of view, his boots thumping so loudly it echoed in the Keep's chamber. The sleeves of his linen shirt flapped as he moved. Anxiety, or perhaps fear, was painted on his exhausted face.

Silvanus walked closer, Havarius still oblivious to his presence. As Silvanus stopped before the mirror, he cleared his throat.

Havarius jumped, eyes wide. "Silvanus! I'm sorry, I didn't see you enter."

Silvanus raised a gentle hand. "Peace, ambassador. The weight upon your shoulders is clear. What troubles you?"

Havarius stopped pacing and crossed his arms, his eyes darting across the floor.

"Where to even begin?" he muttered. "I, I told Caelia about the request after our conversation." Silvanus nodded but remained silent, waiting patiently as Havarius struggled to gather his words. "She didn't have any answers but agreed to help, just like you expected. We snuck into the Firewalker embassy, looking for intelligence Firelord Turgaen sends through Nalindor. But what we found... It's worse than we could have ever guessed."

Silvanus' eyes hardened as he gripped the polished end of his staff. "Go on."

Havarius sighed heavily. "Are you coming for Dragon Day?"

"I have always accepted High King Fael's invitation," Silvanus answered, his curiosity burning.

"Don't come," Havarius blurted with a wild look. "You and the rest of our leaders. Dragon Day. Nalindor. It's all a trap."

"Speak plainly, Havarius. What have you learned?"

Havarius ran a hand through his dark, unkempt hair. "The missing iluvasil from the attack on the Halls? They're here, hidden across Nalindor, along with the Firelord's entire force of Ilumancers. Caelia found an order from him, outlining the Firewalkers' plan to wipe out the Oathsworn *and* the Elves using their power on Dragon Day. The one day everyone is together."

Silvanus' heart nearly stopped beating. His eyes grew large and his mouth ran dry. "Have you any proof?"

"I. No." Havarius slumped against the desk. "Caelia created a diversion so I could escape, and she had the scroll. We have to rescue her!"

"A sleight of hand," Silvanus murmured. "It was never Reachwind. Turgaen, you have been clever."

"They'll wipe out every leader in Andaaya if the Oathsworn come," Havarius exclaimed, stepping closer to the arcane stone. "You *must* stay away."

Silvanus bent his head, his brow furrowed. After a long pause, he looked up at Havarius and smiled. "I have already accepted the Everking's invitation, my friend. It would be quite rude to spurn our host."

Havarius' jaw nearly dropped to the floor. "*Grandmaster!* You can't be serious!"

Silvanus continued smiling. "The Oathsworn delegation this year may be somewhat... muted, I am afraid. It has been a difficult season. But if ever there has been a time to stand beside our oldest allies, it would be now. Would you not agree, ambassador?"

"I... Look, I want to stop the Firewalkers as much as anyone, but with the iluvasil, there isn't a power left in Aldaria that can stop them. They literally have *generations* of magic ready to unleash. Not even the Elves can contain that!"

"There are many powers in the world, Havarius," Silvanus said, his voice dropping. "Some older than Andaaya, older than even Elvendom itself. It shall be upon the fate of Elowë that the greater of these is decided."

"I don't understand."

Silvanus relaxed, his gentle eyes holding Havarius' wild stare. "All shall be explained when I join you in Nalindor. Now, Dragon Day is nearly upon us. I shall make ready to leave Reachwind immediately. Look for my arrival not three weeks hence."

"Yes, sir," Havarius replied, still confused. "But... What about Caelia? What about warning the Elves?"

"By all means, inform High King Fael, but I fear the evidence is not in our favor, for now. In the meantime, we must also pray that a path to the princess is opened." Pity gathered on his weathered face. "Though I fear much shall lie in darkness until the day of trial arrives."

"There has to be a way."

"I hope so, my friend, for all our sakes. I shall see you soon, Havarius."

Havarius bowed, exhaustion flooding him once more. Silvanus nodded, watching as a swirl of bluish haze overtook the iluvimír until Havarius and the study faded into obscurity. He stepped back, exhaling as he relaxed the grip on his staff. Then he turned, exiting the bright chamber and striding swiftly through the Keep. Soldiers, scribes, and messengers leapt out of his way as Silvanus hurried down the corridor towards the tall doorway at the end. He walked through the open timbers without pausing, adjusting to the musty gloom of the war room. Warden-Commander Gorim and Warden Sophia jumped as his staff clattered against the stone, breaking their attention from the papers scattered across the war table.

"Grandmaster," Gorim greeted. "What is it?"

Silvanus stepped beside them, his mind whirling. "The time to reveal our trick has come. I am leaving for Nalindor, alone."

"What of the Dragon Day festivities?" asked Sophia. "The other wardens will leave Calharon and the eastern garrisons soon to join us there."

"Send word to the others all are to hold their positions. Both of you are to remain here as well," Silvanus instructed. "Defend Reachwind Keep for as long as possible should the Firewalkers breach the pass."

Gorim frowned beneath his bushy beard, crossing his massive arms. "Dragon Day has always been a day of rest in this war. You believe the Firewalkers will break this honored tradition?"

"Yes, and now is the moment in which you must trust me, my friends, as I asked once before. I pray the end of this war draws nigh. Yet, should my plans fail, it falls to you to lead our people." He rested a gentle hand on Gorim's tensed shoulder. "Will you do this?"

The warden-commander frowned deeper. Then he grunted, nodding. "As you say, grandmaster. Though I hate to miss the festival."

Silvanus chuckled. "With the Creator's blessing, there shall be many eras of peace and celebration yet to come. Thank you both. Now, I must be off."

"May the Creator guide you," Sophia murmured as together they bowed.

Silvanus swept back down the hall, rushing into his chamber. Into his travel satchel, he shoved his clothes and his collection of writings. Then he plucked Heran's journal from the desk, securing it within the clasped pocket of the bag. Moments later, he returned to the sprawling halls of the Keep, descending the main stairs to the busy courtyard where soldiers scurried, bolstering the defenses along every wall. He strode towards the carriage parked near the edge of the stables, its driver stumbling to salute as Silvanus came to a halt.

"To Nalindor, with haste."

"Ye–yes, sir."

He leapt into the carriage and the horses kicked up a whirlwind of dust. Soldiers scrambled aside as they trotted through the gates, the coach bumping down the trail snaking southeast along the mountains. Silvanus leaned to the window, gazing at the Keep. Its lofty towers gleamed above the verdant plains like majestic pinnacles, defying the doom tightening its grip. He pressed further out the window, his eyes drifting behind and up towards the snowy peaks, receding behind the trees. A pang of grief stabbed his heart.

Creator, forgive me.

Chapter 17
Lost

Time dragged in the endless gloom, the empty silence torment-ing Caelia as much as her own mind. Except for Marlond's routine visits to drop a tray of food on the small table in the center, always in silence, everything else from the gloomy walls to the smell of decay remained unchanged. She laid on the uncomfortable bed, praying for deliverance, hearing only the silence.

Suddenly, the door groaned, opening to reveal the comman-der's dark form. Caelia dragged herself upright, summoning her customary glare. Marlond stepped forward, gesturing towards the hall.

"You will accompany me upstairs, princess," he said in his deep voice. "Try anything and you will regret it. My hauling you to the Firelord will be the least of your worries."

Caelia's gut twisted.

"Well?"

She staggered from the bed, forcing her stiff legs to carry her to the shadowy door. The back of her neck tingled as she passed Marlond, his icy gaze tracking her every move. There was nowhere to run, not now. Not with her father here.

Real light and fresh air swept across Caelia's face for the first time in days as she shambled out of the cellar passage. She drank it in like a starving man entering a feast. For all she knew, that glimpse of the trees and daylight beyond the windows of the manor might be her last. Marlond nudged her, and she marched on.

As they crossed the foyer, empty of all signs of life, that familiar fear crept back into her. Outside the door to her father's study, it threatened to burst from her chest. She almost wished it would. Perhaps it would be more merciful. Marlond thrust open the door.

"Enter."

Her father's voice sent a shiver down her spine. Caelia stepped inside, a brief flash of Havarius crouched beside the door flickering through her mind. Long enough to quell her terror.

He's safe, she told herself. *As long as he's safe.*

Caelia lifted her face from the floor, finding the fire of her father's amber eyes consuming her from across the desk. Marlond followed and closed the study door. Her heart beat faster beneath her expressionless stare. The Firelord gestured to the chair across from him.

"Sit."

Caelia sat.

He stood across the desk, his palms resting on the unblemished wood, as he studied her in silence. She wasn't sure what unnerved her more, his furious gaze or the void between them. She focused on her hands folded in her lap.

"Why?" he finally asked, startlingly calm against the rest of his demeanor. Caelia looked up at him. "You have betrayed the Firewalker Order."

"I did not—"

"You betrayed *me*," he growled.

"Everything I have done has been for the good of our—"

"Lies!" The Firelord slammed a fist against the desk, a spark of flame leaping into the air. "Do not take me for a fool, Caelia. I will not suffer deception. You *will* tell me everything."

Firelord Turgaen stormed around the desk, shoving her chair to face him. Caelia stared at her lap again as he roared over her, "A name, Caelia! *Who did you share it with?*"

Silence.

"The Elves? The Oathsworn?" Turgaen punched the desk beside her, the force shaking the chair. "*Answer me!*"

Caelia lifted her face to meet his, fiery wrath falling against her defiant, piercing glare.

Pain raced across Caelia's cheek and she gasped as her head jerked sideways. Turgaen pulled back his open hand, breathing hard. Tears welled as the warm sting spread across her skin. She forced herself not to raise her fingers to it, blinking the blurring from her sight.

"Insolent child. To think I trusted you as a leader of our order. To have given you a station of prestige and power among us."

"I will not be party to genocide," Caelia hissed. "It's you who are betraying everything I have worked for, everything our people have worked for!"

Turgaen shoved a finger towards her. "Do *not* question my actions. I will not grovel before the spineless lords of Nalindor. Vengeance for generations of the Firewalkers' subjugation will be mine to take! I will not let the likes of you ruin this chance for triumph. The Order will be free from the shackles of lesser men, by whatever means necessary."

Caelia shook her head, tears forming behind the pulsing pain and despair in her heart. "You'll destroy it all, father. This will ruin the Firewalker Order and Andaaya with it."

The Firelord scowled. "You are as blind as you've ever been. Too young and naïve to have embraced the deeper teachings of the Creed. I should have seen it long ago."

"Please... stop this," Caelia begged as he stepped back, gazing at the banner on the wall. "There has to be another way."

Turgaen shook his head. "I will not betray the Order. With the iluvasil and our gift of blood, our mages will be the most powerful force in Aldaria. I will usher in a new era of dominion and rule, untainted by the weakness of the past. And no one, not the Elves, not the Oathsworn, not you and their meddling ambassador, will threaten that ever again."

Caelia's blood ran cold. "What did you say?"

He turned his face to her, his lip curled into a sneer. "I am not blind, Caelia, and you are not as clever as you think. Did you really believe all your nighttime ventures had escaped my notice? I have eyes all across Nalindor now. You read the words yourself."

It felt as if a rock had dropped into her stomach.

"No..."

"Why Silvanus ever chose the young fool is beyond me," he continued. "Arrogant dotard. He ought to have sent the man to die with his father in the mountains."

Caelia jumped from her seat. "You wouldn't," she gasped. "You—"

"Wouldn't? The chance to finally eradicate the Stormcrown name for their part in our sufferings? Oh, I am simply *enthralled* with anticipation."

Marlond stepped behind her, his gauntlets digging into her shoulders as he forced her back into the seat. Her whole body trembled, fear raging with powerlessness. The commander stretched out his hand, passing the scroll to Turgaen, who sauntered to the middle of the study. He unfurled the letter, lingering over the page like a priceless treasure.

"It is beautiful, you know," he murmured, his gaze never leaving it. "Almost poetic. A single, decisive victory, and all of our forefathers' dreams, everything Kanuh promised them... finally realized."

Caelia struggled against Marlond's grip, breathing erratically. "This is madness! The Oathsworn—"

Suddenly, light blossomed in his palm. Flames licked up the edges of the scroll, devouring the dry parchment in seconds. Ashes drifted to the floor as he wiped his hands, smiling.

He turned to Caelia. "The Oathsworn know nothing. It matters not what knowledge you gave to your companion, the *Stormcrown* fool. I know just as much the mind of their Elvish king as you, daughter." His teeth gleamed as he moved closer. "Pompous twit. The Everking will do as he always does: wait and do nothing until it is too late. The word of one novice Eldvenir will hardly be enough to sway the Elves."

Desperate fury rose within her. "They know your plan! They will not stand for this, and you will walk into a trap of your own making!"

Firelord Turgaen stood back, folding his hands behind him as he grinned at Caelia. "Oh, I'm afraid our snare will be quite secure when the festival arrives."

He nodded to Marlond, who forced Caelia to stand. Her legs threatened to fail, every fiber pounding with the force of blood in her veins.

"Return the princess to her chamber. And see that her dress is prepared."

"Yes, my lord."

Caelia stared at her father, stunned. "I will not."

"You will," he calmly replied. "You will prepare yourself before Dragon Day arrives and accompany me to the ceremony, as is tradition. Any act, any thought, of rebellion, and I will ensure that the Stormcrown name vanishes that very hour." She choked back a gasp, drawing a triumphant smile from him. "I thought so. Rest well, daughter. Victory is upon us. You will need your strength."

The Firelord turned back to the desk as Marlond nudged her from the room. Caelia plodded forward, not even glancing up. Her entire world was shattered. No, not just her world. Her heart. Tears streamed down her aching cheek, hidden by the hair shielding her eyes, though she no longer cared who saw. She turned away from the sunlit world beyond her prison and descended into shadows.

Chapter 18

Legends

Laughter echoed from beyond the courtyard as Havarius dashed towards the embassy manor. The driver had barely slowed the horses before he had leapt out, nearly tumbling onto the paved drive.

He has to be here by now. Havarius gritted his teeth, shoving open the door. The heavy timbers slammed into the wall, the crash reverberating fiercely across the lofty atrium. A young maid dusting shelves in the corner jumped in fright. The rest of the entry was empty. Nothing.

"Sorry," he muttered. Then he stomped into the study. Havarius closed the door, a little less abruptly this time, then slumped in the tall, carved chair behind the desk.

Since King Fael relegated his warning to another "investigation," Havarius had tried every idea he could muster to find Caelia. At least, those beyond invading the Firewalker embassy. She had not attended their weekly appearances before King Fael, supposedly feeling unwell, according to their emissaries. Their embassy had summarily expelled the messengers he had sent under the guise of a meeting to resolve complaints involving the refugees. Even his attempts to reach her through the Void while loitering near its grounds, as unskilled in the art as he was, resulted only in ominous silence. With each passing day, his despair grew and his hope waned. Guilt hung over every waking moment.

I left her. Elowë, why did I leave her?

Havarius growled, scattering a stack of papers across the desk. He put his elbows on the polished surface, holding his head in his hands. His ideas were exhausted, his prayers unheeded. In the silence of the dim study, Havarius felt overwhelmingly alone. His breath caught in his throat, his eyes watering.

A knock rapped against the wooden door.

Havarius sat up, startled. "Yes?"

The door gently swung open. Silvanus' gray, unassuming robes filled the entrance, his bright blue eyes gazing at Havarius with deep pity as wrinkled hands tapped his obsidian staff lightly against the floor. Havarius staggered from his seat.

"You made it," he breathed.

"Greetings, ambassador," said Silvanus, stepping into the room. "Forgive my delay. It is a long journey from Reachwind, and when they are not treacherous, the roads are swollen with pilgrims flocking to the heart of the Elves."

"I haven't found her," Havarius mumbled with bitterness. "I'm sorry, I've tried. And King Fael won't act without proof."

Silvanus nodded sadly. "The princess' fate is now joined to ours. I fear she is beyond our reach, save only through conquering the darkness before us."

"But how? Without the Elves, without *something*, how are we going to defeat an army of Firewalkers with limitless power?"

Silvanus wandered towards the narrow window, looking out at the embassy grounds. For some time he was silent, gazing at the peaceful trees, rustling under the sunny skies. He turned to Havarius, his eyes hard and narrowed. His staff tapped once against the tiles. "What do you know of the Dragon Tamers?"

"Um, not much? They're one of the Firewalker legends my instructors always forbade."

"For many reasons. The horrors of blood magic, not least among them."

"I always figured they were fairy tales, made up to frighten Oathsworn initiates. At least, until…"

"Yes," Silvanus murmured. "The crown prince upended more than he knew. For some time, I have feared their likeliness would rise once more. And now we have seen their power confirmed."

"So you really think Dragol found something? Wherever he—"

"He did. The signs are clear."

Havarius crossed his arms. "Alright. What does this have to do with Caelia and Dragon Day?"

Silvanus sighed. "Their legends tell of great mages among the Firewalkers, those possessing terrible powers through the blood. That those who achieve the summit of its might can not only dominate the minds of Man, but even the Bound."

Havarius gaped at him in awe. "But the dragons of Aldaria are the most powerful and intelligent beings in existence. How could—how did—blood magic overcome them?"

"It is hard to say. Though in forsaking the Void and binding themselves to the created order, there is much the Bound relinquished. And there are laws of Elowë that run deeper than the Current itself. Blood is sacred, in it all life finds its source through the Creator. That is the great treachery of blood magic—a warping of the gift Elowë bestowed to serve the pride of Man. In it, the dark spirits whisper we are gods, free to chart our own destiny."

A knot formed in Havarius' stomach. "But not always, right? Can't blood magic be used to serve others, just as the other Paths of magic?"

Silvanus frowned. "Not in the millennia since Kanuh, the Deceiver, persuaded Lornan and revealed the forbidden magic. All who practice it are consumed, enslaved by its power and the spirits of the Deceiver." His expression shifted slightly, relaxing. "Though perhaps now, in the darkest of days, all that once was may give birth to what is new."

Havarius stared blankly at him. "What do you mean?"

"In our time together, I have not perceived the same taint upon you as so many of the Firewalkers display," Silvanus answered. "You have embraced some aspects of the forbidden magic, as was clear in your encounter with the princess." He studied Havarius, who squirmed under his penetrating gaze. "Yet the whispers and its allure have not swayed you, thus I have watched, and waited. Why has it not, I wonder?"

Silvanus paused. "There is something different about the form she has taught you. Something the Firewalkers, perhaps even Kanuh, do not see. And thus, in this our true illusion, our desperate hope, might now be revealed."

"My blood magic?"

"Yes, dear Havarius. Never have I held you in contempt, and now, in you, all my hope is placed. You hold the key, young Eldvenir."

Havarius' eyes widened. "The key to what?"

"The key to saving Andaaya. To becoming the greatest Dragon Tamer the world has ever known. The key to taming a Void-wing."

Havarius' mind exploded with a thousand questions, confusion running rampant in every corner as he paced agitatedly around the room. "I. No. The Void-wing? Blood magic? It, it doesn't make sense. How am I going to stop the Firewalkers with blood magic?"

Silvanus stepped closer, his blue eyes blazing. "Your magic has overcome the darkest temptations, the temporal impulses that enslave. It is through that lust both mortals and Bound alike are snared. Flesh becomes captive to the law it transgressed. But you. The magic you received has transcended those shackles. Its gaze is higher than yourself. High enough perhaps to reach the plane of the Creator himself."

"Wait. You think my blood magic has power over the Void? Over the Creator?"

"Not over Elowë, aligned with him," Silvanus explained. "An expression of magic as attuned in its self-sacrifice as Elowë's Song through the Bound, which created Aldaria itself. And for that reason, potent enough, that one wholly devoted to the Creator might follow its summons."

Realization nearly floored Havarius as he clutched the edge of the desk. "You want to use the Void-wing to defeat the Firewalkers? *Enslave* it?"

Silvanus gently shook his head. "I seek to *persuade* the Void-wing. To use the gift you possess with the power at our disposal as an offering before it and to prove the worth of our plea. Your blood magic is the key to reaching the essence of its being, to make it see the righteousness of our plight."

"I... I don't know," Havarius stammered. "Surely, the Void-wing will see the Firewalkers and their brutality? What about the Everking's prophecy?"

"Havarius, you have lived among the immortal Elves for many years. You have seen their unwillingness, their inaction, however well-intentioned. They are not so far removed from the dragons. I fear the Void-wing shall see our plight no more than they. We must persuade the Void-wing by any means."

Havarius stepped back, rubbing his temple.

"I cannot do this without you, Havarius," said Silvanus quietly. "This is the culmination of all I have done for our people, and to avenge your father. It is up to you."

Havarius jerked his gaze to the wizened man. Silvanus regarded him with a patient, hopeful gleam. Thoughts of Caelia, and of his father, flashed painfully through his mind.

"I'll do it."

Chapter 19
Dragon Day

Banners of rich green and gleaming silver snapped in the evening breeze high above the palace walls. As the sun receded beyond the hennaleth and racing clouds, new light sprang from lampposts dotting a sea of life that shifted between the ancient trees and gleaming spires of Nalindor. Musicians blared from street corners as children shrieked and reunited friends yelled to one another. The carriage inched through the parting crowd of humans and Elves, Havarius shifting restlessly across from Silvanus and leaning out the window for a better view. A dozen scents pummeled his nose—fresh flowers, the sweat of bodies, baked treats, roasted nuts. It was overwhelming.

As the carriage rumbled through the high archway of the courtyard, the crowds pressed tighter, eager faces peering for a glimpse of the wide enclosure lined with sprawling hennaleth as it swept towards the dome of the Great Well. Near the end of the crowd, the carriage circled around and two Elvish soldiers approached, waiting as Silvanus climbed out and Havarius followed.

The escorts guided them through excited rows of onlookers, Havarius scanning the slew of faces nervously. Any number of them could be the secret Ilumancers. He shook his head and focused on the palace steps. He could just make out an array of emerald streamers and bright golden lights lining the balcony overlooking the rest of the courtyard. Silvanus glanced behind as a large man backed into Havarius, nearly knocking him off his feet. Havarius grunted, stumbling towards him.

"High King Fael is expecting us," Silvanus calmly called over the noise. "Be prepared for anything."

Havarius nodded, trailing closely as they approached the row of Elvish soldiers hemming in the crowd at the chiseled stairs. Their bright spears and viridian helms radiated from the lights of the festival, appearing almost joyous. An Elvish captain in engraved armor of shifting gold and emerald stepped forward, bowing before Silvanus. The warriors next to him parted, granting escape from the eager throng. As Havarius mounted the stairs, flutes and lyres echoed over the din, amplified by the enclosing foliage and stone of the massive space. He glimpsed raven hair and a swirl of silver and gold robes as he joined Silvanus at the top. King Fael hurried over, his ageless face beaming with surprise beneath his diamond crown. Silvanus bowed, steadying himself on his staff.

"My friends! Ma Elowë vesir nau oín. This shall be a most joyous day indeed!" King Fael proclaimed. "You humble me, as do so many others who have come to celebrate the Finale of Remembrance, this most momentous of Dragon Days."

Silvanus nodded, stepping closer. "Indeed, my king. Even in trial, the Oathsworn shall never abandon this sacred tradition, nor our closest friends. We are honored to join you, such as we may."

"Allovan'oín, alenon," said King Fael, his brightness fading slightly. "Even should only two of the Eldvenir be our guests, the spirit of your people shall magnify our celebration. The Oath has forever bound us as kindred."

Havarius surveyed the curved balcony, empty save a pair of guards near the ends of the streamers and lights. Five grand seats carved in the likeness of living trees sat behind a small podium overlooking the sea of color that engulfed the palace grounds. Havarius sensed Silvanus stiffen.

"Firelord Turgaen shall be joining us then," said Silvanus, more a statement than a question.

"Yes." The Everking's expressing grew troubled. "Soon, I expect. The moment to begin draws near." He paused, studying the aging mage. Then he stepped closer to Silvanus, lowering his voice. "I must ask once more, alenon, for you to consider my plea. Please, put aside the decades of grievances between Firewalker and Eldvenir. Let Andaaya be healed of its wounds tonight. Hope rises upon the Void-wing. This is a mercy of Elowë, of which we are not worthy." Silvanus narrowed his eyes.

"It is a chance for the Eldvenir to be restored, for the Mantle to be upheld and peace to spread across Aldaria once more," the king pleaded. "Will you trust in this? Will you trust me, as your forbearers have? I long to see this peace for the good of all, for it to be the culmination of all our trials. A final beacon of hope before I make the last voyage. So that I might know the promise we made before Elowë shall continue on, long after I have passed back into the Ageless Realm. Silvanus, my friend, will you renounce your part in this war and appeal for peace?"

Silvanus was unreadable, staring into the eager gray eyes of the Elvish king. Havarius couldn't breathe, hanging on the maddening silence as the sounds of the festival faded.

"No."

King Fael's hopefulness shattered.

"I am sorry, avanuil, my king," Silvanus continued solemnly. "I have trusted you and shall always trust you. There is a great fondness for your people in my heart, and it shall always be so. Yet I cannot in good conscience before the Creator relent of all the Eldvenir have suffered and died for at the hands of our betrayers. In them I place no trust, no hope of a peace for Andaaya until their power and influence is stayed. Until the Elves join us in recognizing the threat they present, the Oathsworn shall do all that is necessary to ensure the peace of Andaaya."

King Fael stepped back, holding his hands together and dipping his head. Havarius felt waves of sadness from the immortal king, moving his own heart as if a reunion with his mother and sister were standing before him and suddenly snatched from his grasp.

"The Firewalkers are a danger," Silvanus warned, "not to the Eldvenir only, but the Elves as well. The word of my ambassador is true. They shall betray you, my king, as their forefathers did mine. Even here, at our most sacred observance, none are safe."

King Fael sighed and looked out at the crowd, growing in its anticipation. The daylight was nearly gone, the strength of the arcane lights growing in the shadows of the trees.

"A pity," he murmured, half to himself. "Ever are my pleas destined for ears that do not hear." He focused back on Silvanus. "My heart is filled with sorrow at your words, alenon. I do not discount the sufferings of the Eldvenir. Yet, I fear suspicion has long festered in your hearts, and that revenge has hardened them. I believed by the words of Turgaen there to be a chance here, tonight, for all to be made right. Were it your heart also softened to the call."

Even as he finished, a dark shaped mounted the stairs across from them. Firelord Turgaen swerved to face them, his black furred cloak and gold-embellished raiment gleaming in the enchanted lights. His eyes darkened, lips turned into a frown within his beard as he spied Silvanus. The Oathsworn froze, locking gazes as wary predators over a kill. Two more shapes clambered up the steps. The first, a tall man in slim, polished armor the color of midnight. Curving patterns of gold crossed his scales and flowed down the cape behind him. His chestnut beard was neatly trimmed, much like the Firelord's, and piercing brown eyes bore into Havarius as he joined his king. Havarius tore his eyes away from the soldier to the last, slender form rounding the stairs.

"Caelia!" Havarius' jaw nearly dropped, his heart leaping at the sight of the unadorned blond waves that obscured her gentle face.

Silence. Havarius felt Silvanus' voice hard and cold in his mind.

Havarius forgot everything else, straining to catch her eye. She kept her gaze down, partially hidden in the growing dusk. King Fael relented, turning to face the Firewalkers.

"Ma Elowë vesir nau oín, Firelord Turgaen. And you, Commander Marlond and Princess Caelia," he greeted warmly.

The Firelord bowed curtly, expressionless. "High King Fael. Apologies for our tardiness. May we begin?"

"Indeed." King Fael beckoned to the seats. The group cautiously stepped towards them as if the ground might at any moment swallow them whole. Commander Marlond claimed the middle, separating Silvanus and Turgaen as Havarius and Caelia were relegated to the ends. Havarius leaned forward as he sat, looking towards her. Just as Caelia took her seat, her beautiful hair shifted and hazel eyes met his. Havarius' hopeful gaze was crushed as he found her hollow stare. She shook her head once, enough for him to catch a change of color below her eye and along her cheek in the gloom. Dismay and fury exploded in his soul. Havarius snapped forward, clenching his jaw and gripped the arms of his seat.

I'll kill him.

The crowd erupted in cheers as King Fael strode onto the podium, overlooking the multitude of smiling faces. The Everking smiled back, raising his hands. Voices and music faded across the courtyard, replaced by eager silence as shadows enveloped the assembly.

"Welcome, people of Andaaya. Welcome to thee of the Elder Souls, and to thee of the First Men, our beloved kindred. We gather here as one, at the root of our past, at the culmination of our Remembrance, at the coming glory of the Creator! Dragon Day is upon us once more!" Cheers ensued, as Havarius forced himself to focus on the king.

"Tonight, we praise Elowë, Father of All, who in love gave life both mortal and immortal. We honor the sacrifice of the Bound, the first dragons through whom all creation was fashioned by him. And we celebrate his heralds, the Void-wings, through whom the voice of Elowë flows as we await the Final Song and the restoration of all the Creator has formed.

"In both peace and hardship, we look to his first creations, remembering their noble example as we uphold the Oath, our promise before the Creator. As one, we pursue our calling under the Mantle of Stewardship, eager for the day when this momentary glimpse into a perfected future becomes our eternal reality. The day when, as one people, united with the earnestness of the Bound and the devotion of the Void-wing, we stand before

Elowë without hesitation and the trials of this mortal realm are redeemed.

"Here, as our Year of Remembrance closes and Dragon Day arrives, we yearn for this, and we rejoice, knowing we are a moment closer to that eternity!"

Thunderous clapping and cries broke from the multitude of Elves and Men. A series of brilliant arcane sparks in a rainbow of colors exploded from the sides of the courtyard, covering the cacophony with the crackle of magic. Havarius noticed Marlond shift in his seat and lean forward. King Fael raised a hand again, but the celebration continued unabated.

Turgaen cleared his throat, loudly enough to draw the Elvish king's attention. "My king, if I may?"

King Fael hesitated before finally gesturing for Turgaen to take the stand. The Firelord rose and bowed, striding to the podium as King Fael stepped back. Havarius saw Silvanus could barely restrain his displeasure. The sounds and fireworks died away, replaced by curiosity.

Turgaen's fierce gaze scanned the audience. "Dear people of Andaaya," he boomed. "It is indeed a blessed day, worthy of our merriment. For there is much to be grateful for, even in these difficult times. For too many years, Andaaya has suffered from endless struggle, endless strife. The Firewalkers have felt the pain of it alongside each of you. So it is fitting that here, on Dragon Day, I proclaim to you a new era, the rising of a new peace as glorious as the flaming sun."

Murmurs rose from the crowd. Firelord Turgaen leaned forward, gripping the white stone railing. Marlond shifted again.

"In the dying of Dragon Day, a new victory rises. The Firewalkers have claimed for you this victory, a new leadership that will forever ensure the future of our glorious nation. Our destiny is secure, my brothers. Rise and join the coming dawn!"

"That is far enough, Turgaen," Silvanus cried, leaping to his feet.

At the same moment, Marlond sprung.

High King Fael twisted in shock to look at Silvanus, only for Marlond's gleaming blade to sink into the folds of his shimmering robe. The king gasped, a crimson stain spreading over silver strands.

"No!" Silvanus howled.

Screams rose from beyond the balcony. Flashes of light erupted across the sea of bodies, blasts drowning out the crowd. Havarius watched in horror as the Everking slumped to the ground, lifeless.

"Murderer!" Silvanus roared, raising his palm. Lightning crackled across the platform. In the blink of a moment, the charge slammed into an unseen wall, twisting through the air in every direction. The Firelord stood facing Silvanus, his hand raised as a white shard glowed from a cord half tucked into the fold of his vest.

"Iluvasil," Havarius gasped.

Dismayed cries and stomping boots echoed up the stairs as the Elvish guards at the platform's corners rushed towards the two Firewalkers. Below, the festive courtyard transformed into a charred battlefield. Overturned carts and flaming banners littered the glistening stone. Bodies of Elves and Men lay scattered. A scattering of Elvish soldiers leapt into a furious battle with an army of Firewalker mages, the Ilumancers unleashing towering torrents of flame and lightning.

Silvanus pulled back, readying another blow as Marlond turned to face the Elves. Turgaen's hateful eyes never left his rival. Silvanus paused, long enough for another contingent of Elves to swarm the stairs behind Havarius, flowing to meet the Firelord.

"Not here," Silvanus muttered, lowering his hand. He turned to Havarius. "Come, quickly!"

As the Elves unleashed whirlwinds and blizzards at the encircled pair, Havarius chased after Silvanus, already at the palace gates.

"Wait! Caelia!" Havarius frantically scanned the balcony, straining for a glimpse of her in the chaotic battle as a viridian sea surrounded the Firewalkers.

"There's no time," Silvanus barked.

Havarius growled and sprinted into the shadowed halls.

Chapter 20
The Cataclysm

Havarius' boots pounded against the plush floor of the corridor, its tranquil gardens broken by echoing blasts and screams beyond the palace gates. Silvanus' dusky robes rippled as the old mage sprinted ahead of him and disappeared around the next corner.

How does he move so fast? Havarius wondered, panting.

Havarius swerved to follow, the chandelier of arcane lights above quaking as an explosion shook the corridor. He bolted down another hall coated with foliage, then another. The sounds of fighting faded the deeper into the palace they ran. At last, Havarius rounded a turn, stumbling into a lofty atrium lined with polished columns chiseled in the likeness of a great forest of white stone. A set of colossal gates waited at the end, flanked by tall flameless lights. The gates' towering timbers were inlaid with gold and silver, etched in designs similar to those of the palace entry, where Elves and other creatures frolicked across the unblemished wood. Silvanus stood before them, breathing hard. Havarius rushed over, still captivated by the majesty of the hall. He couldn't recall the last time he stood here. Perhaps not since his own Joining.

"Is it here?" Havarius wheezed, steadying himself.

"No, but dusk is upon us. We must hurry."

With a flick of his wrist, Silvanus unsealed the massive doors. Havarius watched in wonder as the gates silently opened, beckoning to their visitors. A pure, vivid light flooded the atrium, and Havarius shielded his eyes. Together, the pair crossed into the room.

Havarius' awe spiraled as he gazed at the immense, perfectly rounded chamber, with its walls of gleaming stone stretching stories above them. The domed ceiling appeared as if great branches of petrified hennaleth wove together in an intricate canopy, sealing the room from the world beyond. The lustrous marbled floors gradually stepped down towards the center, where a ring of pure silver engraved with flowing branches encircled the source of the blinding light.

"The Great Well," Havarius breathed.

An immense column of unbroken light spiraled towards the heavens. The air hummed with energy, pulsing in Havarius' head though the chamber was silent. An unspeakable, ancient power emanated from the beam, unlike anything Havarius had ever felt. He knew the lore—of the Well's connection to the Ageless Realm, perhaps even to the City of Elowë itself. Yet it still felt entirely unknowable, making his heart clench at the thought of what was about to come.

Silvanus motioned him on, slowly stepping towards the Well. The air tingled and hairs on his arms raised as Havarius neared the silver ring, almost forgetting to breathe. They stopped mere paces from the light, and Havarius glanced at him. Silvanus looked back, determination spread across his face, and nodded.

"Fools!"

They both swerved around. Firelord Turgaen stood in the massive entrance, the hall behind reduced to a black void beyond the rays of the Well. He scowled at the Oathsworn, fury blazing in his amber eyes. A long, gleaming sword twitched at his side, splattered with blood.

"The Great Well cannot save you," Turgaen hissed, striding closer. "The Everking is dead, and the Elves broken. There is no communion to the Realm beyond left to you."

Silvanus stepped forward, glaring. "You are blind, as you have always been, Turgaen. You think you have won? No. You have betrayed our Creator and damned Andaaya to a future of chaos and destruction. Your actions bring ruin upon us all!"

Turgaen laughed. "*Us*? There is no 'us', Oathsworn. And soon, there will be no 'you'. Reachwind falls as we speak, and once I am finished here, my Ilumancers will march upon Calharon and *finally* rid the world of your name. The Oathsworn are dead. The Firewalkers will rise, and we will drag the world into glory of our own making, free of Elves, Oathsworn, or any others that dare defy our greatness."

Silvanus raised his staff and Havarius watched as it transformed from its simple form into a curving blade of shimmering obsidian metal. Havarius pulled his own blade from the scabbard at his side, stepping beside him.

"The Eldvenir still draw breath," Silvanus growled. "Your conquest ends here, Turgaen."

The Firelord's smug grin shifted to a sneer. "You have no hope, old man. All the power in the world is at my command."

Turgaen raised his hand and unleashed a storm of lightning. The Oathsworn lunged to the sides as the torrent slammed into the Well, veins of blue rippling across the surface before dissipating. Silvanus leapt to his feet, sprinting towards the Firelord as he reached out a hand. The ground quaked and split as a boulder erupted from the floor and barreled at his attacker. Turgaen jerked his arm, and the rock exploded in a cloud of dust. Havarius stepped closer and thrust out his hand, a bolt of flame leaping from his fist. With unnatural speed, the Firelord shifted, and the bolt sailed harmlessly past. But it was enough for Silvanus to close the distance, and the clash of steel rang through the chamber. The pair exploded in a blur of movement, enhanced by the magic coursing through their limbs. Silvanus flowed around his larger opponent, jabbing and dodging blows, but he could not overcome the ferocity of Turgaen. The Firelord was a wall of black and steel, blocking each blow and refusing to give ground.

Silvanus slashed at his side, and Turgaen shoved the blade away with his own. He jabbed his open hand towards Silvanus, unleashing a blast of air that sent the mage stumbling back. Havarius dashed forward, striking at their foe. Their swords echoed across the stone as the Firelord's hateful gaze bore into him.

"You," Turgaen growled, his teeth gleaming. "To think my daughter betrayed me—betrayed everything—for *you*." He laughed wickedly. "Oh, I will enjoy watching you die."

Havarius shoved against his sword, and they sprung apart. He raised his hand, sending out a cone of ice. The blizzard curled around the Firelord's unseen barrier, enveloping him in the freeze. Lightning crackled beside Havarius, and he glanced over as Silvanus unleashed a stream, melding into the swirling storm. Havarius could feel the magic's draw as his limbs grew cold and weakened. Suddenly, the storm exploded, tossing them backwards as ice and bolts scattered into the air. Havarius looked up in shock as the Firelord smirked at them, trickles of blood seeping through his raised fist.

Blood magic.

Havarius clambered to his feet just as a towering inferno lit the room, racing straight towards him. He called on the Current again, forming a barrier just as the flames engulfed him. The blaze slammed into him, shoving him back as energy leeched from his body. He staggered to a knee. *He's too strong!*

The flames vanished, and Havarius looked up to see a storm of lightning crackling around the Firelord. Silvanus shuffled forward, holding out his hands as the stream continued to race across the chamber. Once more, Turgaen's barrier burst, sending the Oathsworn stumbling. The Firelord stretched out his bleeding palm and unleashed a monstrous wave of flames, which was quickly met by a wall of solid stone that collapsed on the blaze, snuffing out the heat whipping Havarius. Silvanus rushed again, his dark sword clanging against Turgaen's as they whirled. Havarius sprang to his feet and raced towards them just as a blast of flames erupted from Turgaen, sending Silvanus flying. With inhuman speed, the Firelord turned and caught Havarius' blade against his. Havarius slashed, meeting Turgaen's again. He feinted, switching to a low cut across his front. The Firelord parried, growling, and stepped back.

A whirlwind smacked Havarius in the chest, and he flailed as his feet left the ground. His back slammed into the floor, stars dancing as the breath was ripped from his lungs. In an instant, Turgaen was upon him, his sword raised. A gleam of light stole his attention and he paused, flicking his hand just as a fireball entered Havarius' view. The flames scattered, and Turgaen shot back a storm of lightning that spread in every direction. Havarius watched in horror as the shower slammed into

Silvanus' barrier, tossing the mage against the far wall. Turgaen snapped back to Havarius, squirming on the ground. He raised his gleaming blade as Havarius fumbled to find his own. Just as the blade's thirsty edge fell, a gust whipped against him, and the Firelord stumbled. Havarius stared, dumbstruck, as Turgaen fell forward, landing hard on the ground next to him.

Havarius scrambled away onto his knees, scanning wildly. "Caelia!"

Caelia stood where her father had been, her arm outstretched. A glowing, white stone hung from a pendant in other her hand, illuminating the golden lines on her emerald dress. Her gentle face was deathly serious, her eyes flickering between Havarius and Turgaen. The Firelord coughed and jumped to his feet as Havarius staggered to his own. Turgaen patted wildly around his vest, then wheeled to his daughter, seething.

"*What is the meaning of this*? How dare you betray me again! For this, this filth!" He cast a venomous look at Havarius. Then he stepped menacingly towards Caelia.

"I showed you mercy when you faced a traitor's due," Turgaen roared. "I gave you *everything*. The power worthy of kings. You would turn your back on the Firewalkers? On your own father?"

She lowered her hand but was resolute, glaring at him. "You haven't been my father for years," she whispered. "My father disappeared the day my mother died."

"How dare you! You insolent child!"

"It's like I'm not your daughter at all," Caelia yelled, clutching the iluvasil tighter. "You treat me like one of your failed officers, discarding me the moment I disappoint you. And no matter how much I've tried to please you, it's never enough. You make me feel useless, like I'll never measure up to your standard. Like I don't matter at all."

"Then you have learned *nothing*," he hissed, scowling. "I expected you to excel, to dominate your circumstances, as Dragol has. Instead, you have allowed yourself to wallow in self-pity. I will be sure to rectify that."

Turgaen lunged for the pendant, and Caelia stepped back, throwing up her hand and blowing him onto the floor. Caelia twisted her wrist and the ground rippled. Bubbling streams of rock rolled across Turgaen's struggling arms and legs, pinning him to the marbled stone. But he could not break the bonds held by the might of the iluvasil gleaming in her fist.

The Firelord roared in fury. "Traitorous girl! I will strip you of everything! You will rot in a cell while your brother and I conquer Aldaria. Insubordinate fool!"

Turgaen squirmed against the shackles as Caelia turned to Havarius, emotionless. He ran to her, gripping her shoulders as he looked her over, lingering on the bruise on her otherwise perfect cheek. "It's nothing."

"Let me," he offered, raising a gentle hand to her face. She grabbed his wrist.

"No, not this time," she said firmly. "Right now, I need the reminder. But, thank you." She leaned forward, kissing him lightly above his jaw. Turgaen roared again. Caelia glanced at him, narrowing her eyes.

"I don't know how long I can maintain the spell," she said, returning to Havarius.

He looked towards the Well. "There's something I have to do. I can stop him, stop all of this, right here."

She nodded. "I trust you." He sighed and squeezed her hands.

Havarius turned around as Silvanus limped over to them. The floor rumbled, causing Havarius to jump. Everyone peered at the Great Well. Havarius crossed the debris-strewn chamber, standing next to Silvanus beside the column of light. Silvanus closed his eyes and breathed deeply.

"He comes."

A low sound barely at the edge of hearing echoed from the Well.

It grew louder.

Havarius stared at the light, straining for a glimpse through the impenetrable wall.

"When he arrives, you must begin the ritual," Silvanus murmured.

"He?"

"Direct your focus towards his mind. You must overcome the barrier. Then I shall meld with your thoughts and together, speak our influence over him." Silvanus slipped his hand into the pocket of his robe.

The vibrations in the air muddied Havarius' vision as the chamber shook, the low hum reverberating as the Current of the world roiled like a boiling sea.

For a second, everything stopped.

A blast of energy erupted from the Well, nearly knocking Havarius off his feet. A massive shape soared through the light, obstructing the column as it broke the surface. The dark form stretched beyond comprehension, widening with each moment until Havarius feared it would breach the chamber. As his vision steadied, Havarius watched with wonder as the form sharpened, transforming into a golden mass. Wings as wide as houses with rich, leathery skin stretched from either side of its glittering torso. Massive legs, thicker than the atrium columns and the color of pure gold, dangled towards Havarius as the dragon circled the Great Well. It stretched its towering neck as it descended, powerful jaws large enough to crush a ship flexing as it shook its pearly horns. The Void-wing glided onto the stone as softly as a gentle rain, coiling its spiked tail around the Well.

"Havarius!"

Havarius woke from his stupor, grasping for the dagger at his side. He brought it to his trembling palm. The Void-wing's deep, yellow eyes snapped onto him. He pulled the blade across his flesh, feeling the pain and exhilaration as blood welled from the wound. Immediately, an explosion of energy rushed upon him, pulling him from his aching body.

"Havarius, *no!*" screamed Caelia.

As he merged the spark of his own life force with the blood's immeasurable power, his thoughts delved into the Void, immersing into the stream of energy cutting through the Current. It flooded towards a brilliant, foreign presence like moths before a torch, crashing into an unseen wall, preventing him from advancing.

This place is not your own, little one, a deep, rumbling voice echoed in his head.

The words fell like stones thrown into a well, rippling with an unspeakable intelligence and ancientness. It shook him to his core.

He pushed harder, feeling the barrier bend beneath the colossal strength of the blood. Suddenly, it dissolved, and Havarius stumbled into a vast, alien consciousness. It was unlike any mind he had ever felt, as if the presence was before him yet everywhere at once.

You should not be here, the dragon's voice rumbled.

Who are you? Havarius dared to ask, searching for its source.

Angoladan. Herald of Elowë, Keeper of the City. I see your thoughts, little one. You know not the Deep Magic your actions shall awaken.

Even within the Void, Havarius could feel a knot forming in his gut. *We need your help.*

Havarius! came Silvanus' cry. A new presence swept towards them, coursing with power. Although Havarius had always felt Silvanus' strength, now it was as if he was there plus ten thousand of himself. *Now!*

Silvanus' weight crashed upon the Void-wing, the dragon's presence swallowed by the torrent of energy. Havarius shook away his doubts and leapt into the flood, melding the potency of his blood with it as the creature pushed against the onslaught. As powerful as it was, Silvanus' might was insurmountable. Havarius felt the dragon's presence lessening, bound in the dominating might of their thoughts as Silvanus channeled their force.

The fate is sealed, came a whisper. *Consumed shall Andaaya be.*

The Void-wing's presence vanished.

Havarius found himself thrust violently from the Void, his body slamming into the ground as his head cracked against the stone. His vision blurred and he groaned, rolling to his side. Silvanus was in a similar state, gasping feebly on the floor. Havarius sat up, dazed. He could hear Caelia screaming, but muffled as if far off. Then he noticed the Well.

The column of light trembled and stuttered, and the chamber shook violently. The dragon's body was writhing around the Well, its golden sheen fading. Energy hummed erratically, as if the Current itself was shattering.

"Havarius," Caelia screamed again. He turned groggily, searching. She slammed into his back, dragging him to his feet. "*What did you do*?" she yelled over the tumult with a horrified expression, shaking him. "This isn't what I taught you! How could you use our magic like that? Like my father would?"

A roar pierced the room. Havarius jerked towards the writhing dragon, now almost an ashen gray. A moment later, Havarius flew through air and slammed into a jut of rock. Pain lanced across his back as he slumped onto the floor. He looked up at the faltering light.

A gush of sickly, pale blue fog spewed from the Great Well, and its light vanished.

The fog swarmed over the Void-wing, obscuring it from sight. It roared again, shaking the fractured chamber. Havarius clambered to his feet, his whole body aching. The fog was spreading across the room. Caelia was nowhere to be seen. Suddenly, a hand dug into his shoulder, shoving him to the ground.

"Your life is mine, *Oathsworn*," Turgaen's voice hissed in his ear as the fog enveloped them.

Then Turgaen gasped. Havarius struggled out of his grip as the Firelord clutched at his throat. Havarius watched in shock as the man struggled for air, kicking wildly. The Firelord's fury turned to terror as he looked helplessly at Havarius. His gasps slowed and limbs stilled.

The Firelord stopped moving.

Havarius crept over to him, feeling for a pulse. Nothing.

Havarius looked at the eerie fog oozing its way past the warped doors of the chamber. *Oh no. What have I done?*

"Havarius!" came Silvanus' coughing voice through the haze. The beaten mage staggered out of the gloom, covered in cuts and bruises. He stopped short as he noticed Turgaen's body.

"I think it was this fog," Havarius rasped. "He just started choking, then... Silvanus, what is going on?"

Silvanus was silent, gazing at the Firelord and leaning heavily on his staff.

"What did we do?"

"We must go," Silvanus said quietly.

"I have to find Caelia."

"She has fled," Silvanus replied in a harder voice. "Havarius, we must move. Now."

He stretched out a hand, pulling Havarius to his feet. Havarius wobbled for a moment before they picked their way through the debris and sickly cloud towards the high doors. Havarius could barely see as they stumbled into the atrium. The fog had obscured everything in a deep, bluish haze. They slowly felt their way down the corridors of the palace, Silvanus summoning a small orb of light in the now-darkened space. The thickness of the mist made it nearly impossible to see beyond a few feet in front of them. The palace was ominously still, not even the echo of battle reaching them. After a while of inching their way forward, they found the first turn and quickened their pace. The unnatural fog drifted through the silent hall, swirling over the foliage along the walls. Only a few scattered orbs from the chandeliers were functioning, flickering like erratic beacons.

A scream pierced the dark.

They exchanged a glance, Havarius gripping his sword tighter. They hurried on, rushing desperately for anywhere free of the swirling taint. Slowly, the consuming fog lessened, and Havarius could glimpse what he knew to be the great gates of the palace. A series of screams, clangs of steel, and howls pierced the gloom. They ran towards the opening.

It is done.

Havarius stumbled to a halt, peering back into the swirling darkness.

Andaaya has fallen.

Chapter 21
Escape

The haze only increased in eeriness as Havarius and Silvanus emerged from the desolate palace. Under the twinkling stars and cover of night, the bluish fog glowed with an unnatural presence, as if it were alive and watching their every movement. Another scream echoed from beyond the palace grounds. Havarius shuddered.

"Come," Silvanus murmured. "I sense the Elves are dwindling, and scattered, but the Void is... unclear. We must reach the embassy and find our people. We shall regroup before the Firewalkers return."

They crept forward, making their way past the bodies of Elves and Firewalkers and down the palace stairs. As they crossed the courtyard, bathed in fog, Havarius stumbled over a soft mound. He glanced down, then stifled a gasp. A slew of corpses—Elvish guards and human civilians—were strewn across the fractured tiles. In the center of one group, a large, fur-covered corpse lay sprawled, gouged with spears. The surrounding guards were covered in gashes, and blood oozed from deep wounds where chunks of flesh had been ripped or bitten off between their fractured armor. Havarius inched closer to the beast. It was easily taller than any man or Elf he knew, with elongated limbs and five razor-sharp claws at the ends of its furry hands. Rings of dark, bare skin encircled its small beady eyes that, even when dead, gleamed with untold rage. Its long snout ended at a dark nose above rows of wicked fangs, smeared with blood.

"I don't think the Firewalkers are coming back," Havarius muttered, nudging the beast. "What is this thing?"

Silvanus joined him, staring at the monster. "I do not know."

A string of shrieks and crashes jerked their gazes towards the shrouded city. Silvanus spun in their direction. "Quickly!"

They stumbled into the silent streets of Nalindor, obscured almost entirely in the accursed cloud. They turned northwards, using the palace walls as a reference, heading for the upper city. Havarius felt as if the smothering vapors had wiped away all life in the world, leaving the pair as the last survivors of some unspeakable calamity. He shivered.

After crossing several intersections, Havarius spied a familiar estate and bakery facing each other across a desolate road. A golden light flickered in and out of existence from a solitary lamppost on the far corner.

"Finally," Havarius breathed. "We're not far from the embassy. Just a few—"

A chorus of howls and yells split the silence ahead of them, followed by more crashes. Havarius whipped out his sword as Silvanus raised his own. More shouts echoed down the empty road as they stepped closer.

"Back, back!" came a voice.

A long, wailing howl pierced the sky. A man screamed as snarls broke out. Silvanus bolted towards a narrow path between two prominent buildings, their pale stone glistening in the fog and strengthening moonlight. Havarius raced after him. The snarls and clang of metal grew louder.

Suddenly, Havarius burst through the cloud into a wide square lined with piles of burning wood that scattered the unnatural fog. In the center, a mass of steel and mottled fur swirled furiously. Then Havarius finally grasped what his eyes saw. He caught the viridian gleam of Elvish armor, lashing out with bolts of fire and fierce swords at more of the terrible, wolfish beasts. Elves and monsters littered the cobblestone, the firelight flickering off slicks of blood. The battered warriors were surrounded, a pack of beasts slinking around the circle on their four skinny limbs as other hulking monsters reared up, swiping at the group with fearsome claws. The wolves yelped and howled, eager for flesh.

Silvanus raised a hand. Great flames lit the square, swallowing the wolves at the back and startling the pack. Their high-pitched shrieks rang in Havarius' ears as the smell of burnt hair and flesh filled his senses.

"To me, Elves of Nalindor," Silvanus bellowed. The pack drew back, a pair leaping towards him. Again, he pushed out an arm and the ground exploded, a pillar of rock launching the first beast high into the air, and it vanished in the fog. Havarius sprang forward, sending a spear of ice into the chest of the other as it bounded over a pile of rubble. The heavy beast tumbled onto the stone, lifeless. The Elves shouted, swarming the remaining pack, who hesitated at this newfound resolve. They scattered, whining and yelping as wolves dashed into the sickly fog, thumps and scrapes of claws fading into the gloom.

As the Elves regrouped and saw to their wounded, one of them came forward. His majestic armor, engraved with the golden lines, was scratched and dented. Grime covered his fair face, but his piercing green eyes blazed with eagerness.

"Allovan'oín, my friends," he said, bowing deeply. "I am Vralsír, Captain of Nalindor and servant of the high king."

"Oín su remon," Silvanus replied, as he and Havarius returned the gesture. "What has happened here? Where are the Firewalkers and the rest of the high king's warriors?"

"The Firewalkers betrayed us," the Elf answered, trembling with anger. "They converged upon the festival, and we were unprepared. Some newfound power was with them, overwhelming our magic. In the midst of battle, this strange mist appeared. Some say it came from the palace itself, though my eyes did not witness this. Suddenly, my kin and the Men around me began to collapse as if slain by invisible foes. The Firewalkers panicked, retreating into the city. Then, these strange beasts began rising out of the cloud, striking down anyone in sight. Scores of citizens now lie slain in the streets."

"They came from the fog?" Havarius echoed.

"Not from this... this Mist," another Elf spoke up. They turned as the bloodied warrior hobbled closer, leaning heavily on a splintered plank. "My eyes have seen a terrible evil. These monsters, they are *us*. Mortals were... transformed... within the courtyard. I swear before the holiness of Elowë, I have seen this."

Silvanus' eyes grew wide. "Transformed?"

"Yes, Eldvenir. I have seen it. The Mist is a curse upon us all."

Havarius felt as if a weight had crushed his stomach. "Silvanus..."

"How far has the fog spread?" Silvanus demanded.

"We are unsure," the Elvish captain admitted. "It has grown beyond the walls of Nalindor, but our sight cannot pierce its fumes."

They stood for several moments in silence, shifting nervously.

"There are few of us left," he added quietly. "Even now, I sense my kindred fading. We cannot hold Nalindor. The beasts are too many."

Silvanus nodded. "We must warn the other cities. Can you help us reach the embassy?"

"Yes. Then my company shall make for Ostinlaë, and warn our remaining councilors."

"Allovan'oín. Let those of your kin you can reach know, so word may be spread."

The captain roused the company, and together, the group hurried back to the street, the groping fog smacking against Havarius' face and sending a chill through his limbs as they delved into its depths once more. More howls echoed through the pale spires and shadows of the hennaleth looming above.

What have I done?

"They're gone," said Havarius, hurrying down the embassy steps and into the courtyard. The tall windows of the manor were dark, its stone glinting in the moonlight. The Elvish warriors shifted anxiously in the shadows, several peering towards the yawning opening to the street, obscured in darkness and Mist.

Silvanus dipped his head. "If the Firewalkers had not already, the Mist likely scared them away. We shall pray they made it safely beyond the city. What of the iluvimír?"

"No response. But that doesn't mean anything. Turgaen could have been lying, or..."

"Reachwind is in the hands of the Creator now," said Silvanus gently. "We must see to what is before us."

Havarius grunted and clomped towards the stables at the far side. He returned a moment later, frowning. "Horses are gone."

Silvanus turned to the Elvish captain. "Captain Vralsír, it would seem we, too, are cut off from our kindred. I fear time does not offer the luxury of a westward journey."

Vralsír nodded. "Ostinlaë is only a day's march east. I have heard from others through the Void that the Mist appears to be spreading more to the west, away from the coast. Those who can shall join us on the road."

"Then it is time we leave Nalindor, for now," Silvanus said. Despair filled the faces of many Elves as their captain turned to them.

"With me, brothers. We make with haste for Ostinlaë to protect the rest of our people. Pray that Elowë be with us."

The company marched silently from the embassy grounds. At the gates Havarius paused, glancing wistfully at the manor shrouded in shadows and sickly Mist. It had been his home for almost half his life. Filled with so many memories of his father, of their life among the Elves. His sanctuary, a refuge among the bustle of the great city and dangers of war. And it had kept his deepest secrets and strongest loves. A sudden loneliness smote his heart.

Caelia.

"Havarius?" Silvanus placed a tender hand on his shoulder. Havarius sighed, pushing back his anguish. Silvanus gazed at him with firm but sympathetic eyes. "We shall return, Havarius. This is not the end of Nalindor, nor of the Oathsworn."

"Aye." Havarius trudged after him, watching as the quiet walls of his home were swallowed in the night.

After an hour of sneaking through the eerie streets and tensing at every chorus of howls, the company came to the wide square before the northern gates of the city. Havarius knew from memory where they were, but the Mist was so thick that the great gates across the cobblestone street were hidden from sight. They peered from the shadows of the buildings, scanning the area for any signs of life. Vralsír motioned to his warriors, and a pair slipped noiselessly into the dim moonlight. Swiftly, they stole across the exposed square, fading into the sickly fog.

A howl broke from the veil, followed by shouts.

"To me," Vralsír yelled. The company sprang from the darkness, racing through the Mist as steel rang against stone. More howls split the air.

A voice cried out and Havarius sprinted blindly towards it. Instantly, the hulking mass of a wolf materialized in the haze. It reared on its hind legs, looming over a scout as he frantically dragged himself away. Havarius roared, leaping with his sword outstretched. The monster spun around with incredible speed. The blade plunged into the beast's chest as claws scraped against Havarius' shoulder. Searing pain raced across his back as the wolf gasped and toppled, dragging Havarius down with it. He landed on its hardened torso, the smell of dank, musty fur pressing into his nostrils. Havarius hobbled to his feet and pulled the sword from its abdomen, wiping blood on its matted fur. He could feel his own wound seeping into the fabric of his tunic as he turned and helped the Elf to his feet.

"Allovan'oín, alenon," he breathed, fetching his blade from the ground.

"Are you hurt?" Havarius asked, grasping at the pain in his shoulder.

"My wound is small, smaller than yours, at least. Please, allow me, alenon."

The Elf moved behind Havarius and placed his bare palm over the wound. Havarius winced at the pressure. A brief glow sprang from the shadows, followed by relief like icy water poured across his back. The warrior stepped away and Havarius stretched. The pain was gone.

"Your skin is healed, though it needs more time to repair its deeper flesh. Be careful, friend."

"Thanks," said Havarius, grinning. "I'd say we're even."

More howls erupted from the Mist and they looked back.

"The gates!" Vralsír called through the dark. "Make for the gates!"

"Come on!"

They sprinted on, shapes rising from the deathly fog as the pair joined the other warriors. The pale glow of the Mist grew darker.

More howls rang out, closer.

Suddenly, the high walls of Nalindor rose from the shadows like a black cage. A narrow strip of glowing fog split through the darkness before them.

Havarius glanced behind as more shapes emerged from the Mist. "Wolves!"

A massive wolf sprang upon the group, dragging an Elf to the ground, screaming. Havarius watched in horror as it sank its fangs into his exposed neck, claws tearing at his armor.

Havarius stopped, shoving both hands towards the lumbering mass of beasts. He pulled on the Current, drawing deeply from the stream of magic. A column of flames burst forth, Mist scattering like leaves before a storm as the inferno rocketed into the pack. Shrieks and yelps drowned the square, and the monsters scattered, slinking into the obscurity of the displaced fog.

"Havarius!" Silvanus yelled from the gates. Havarius turned and dashed through the narrow opening between the doors, just as the leading beasts sprang after him. Silvanus grunted, spreading his arms. The earth trembled and the gates shuddered. A wall of solid rock split through the cobblestone of the square, blocking Havarius' view of the beasts. Silvanus pulled his arms closer, and the slab rumbled against the gates, shoving the massive timbers together.

BANG!

The gates of Nalindor slammed shut as the boulder toppled. Havarius gripped his knees, breathing hard, as his adrenaline failed and the toll of magic seeped the strength from his limbs. Weakly, he scanned the bare road and leafy trees rustling in the moon's light as tendrils of Mist swirled in their branches.

"I hope no one else tries this way," Havarius wheezed as Silvanus shuffled closer. The old mage nodded somberly.

Together they joined the Elvish warriors, gazing pensively at the sweeping walls. Havarius felt a pang of sadness as he observed their downcast faces. They had all lost their home now. Who knew if any would return?

As one, the Elves turned from the forsaken city, fading into the dark. Havarius and Silvanus followed as the Mist swallowed them in its nebulous depths.

Chapter 22
Ostinlaë

Dawn's frail warmth spread across Havarius' skin, chasing away the chill of night. He rubbed his eyes, blinking as the bright sun slipped over the trees. The Oathsworn and Elves had barely paused in their moonlit march, plodding resignedly along the road as it grew dustier and hillier the further east they trekked. Another small group of Elvish warriors had joined with them not far from Nalindor, more battered survivors thankful enough to receive Captain Vralsír's message. Silvanus and Havarius trailed the despondent company in silence. Havarius gazed at their sagging shoulders, listening to the sad clinking of dulled armor now razed of its once-majestic luster.

Havarius' stomach churned as the Void-wing's words echoed in his mind. For hours now, he had relived the encounter at the Great Well, struggling to make sense of it all. How had their hope of pleading with the dragon gone so terribly wrong so fast? What had his blood magic done? And that massive wave of power...

He glanced at Silvanus, shuffling ahead of him.

He said he wanted to influence it, Havarius mulled. *But did he, really?*

Doubt gnawed at him, fueled by his own guilt.

By mid-morning, the last vestiges of the Mist had relinquished their grip on the world, the nightmarish fog dissipating as they broke from the deep forest of Nalindor and into sweeping plains of high grass and sparse trees. Everyone's spirits lifted noticeably, and their unbowed pace quickened. Yet, even below the bright, clear sun, shadows grew in Havarius' heart. Everything he knew, everything he had sworn to uphold, felt as false as the peace of the plains and their ignorance of the destruction brewing at their borders.

As evening fell and daylight faded, the exhausted company could feel the city nearing. Seagulls cried overhead, gliding eastward on the faint breeze. The air felt fresh and moist. What still unsettled Havarius, though, was the lack of travelers. All day, the road had remained barren. No panicked festivalgoers racing from behind, no traders or Elves rambling their way towards the Elvish capital. Their group seemed conspicuously out of place in the consuming solitude.

At last, the group crested a wide hill of grass swaying like a sea of gold. Havarius breathed deeply, salt and the cries of gulls rising over the fronds. Below him, a city of polished towers and curving domes glittered against the endless blue of the sea. Great trunks and green boughs twisted among silver spires, as if the port had grown from the earth itself, nestled among a garden of the Creator. Gentle, golden lights pulsed through the windows and into the streets, whispering welcome and respite to the spent warriors.

"Ostinlaë," Silvanus murmured. Havarius jumped as he appeared beside him. "It has been too long since my gaze fell upon its beauty, and that of the sea."

"Do you think they know?"

Silvanus shrugged. "Perhaps. Others who traveled for Dragon Day may have returned. Regardless, we must see to the Order." He paused, watching from the corner of his eye as the Elves passed by. "There is a group of Eldvenir in the city at my command. We must contact them immediately."

Havarius raised a brow. "What are they doing here?"

"Our plan to reach the Void-wing was not my only defense against the Firewalkers. It may be the knowledge here is all that stands between our people and annihilation under the Mist."

Silvanus started walking after the others, but Havarius hesitated. "Silvanus." The wrinkled mage turned back, leaning on his staff. "What happened at the Well? Did you speak to Angoladan?"

Silvanus paused. "I did what I believed would best ensure our people's survival."

"That's not what I asked."

"Come. Night is nearly upon us."

The wizened mage resumed his walk towards the city, gleaming in the gathering dark. Havarius clenched his fist and marched silently after him.

They caught the Elves just before the entrance to Ostinlaë. Captain Vralsír stood patiently before an extravagant archway of white, unblemished stone. The main street ran towards the ocean, surrounded by an expanse of radiant buildings and breathtaking flora.

"Grandmaster Silvanus, Ambassador Havarius," Vralsír said, bowing. "I thank you for your help in saving my brothers. Were it not for your valor, many may never have beheld the glorious sight of our sister city."

"Allovan'oín, captain," Silvanus replied. "We are indebted to you for your courage and bravery. I fear it is here our paths diverge. We must make ready to warn the other Eldvenir, as you must your own."

Vralsír nodded sadly. "Indeed. Even in the presence of our kin, despair grows in my heart. I must see the councilors, so those of us who remain may—"

"Halt!"

Everyone jumped as a force of Elves surrounded the company, their bows raised. An Elf with serious eyes in armor similar to Vralsír's strode from the ring, staring directly at the Oathsworn.

"What is the meaning of this, brother?" Vralsír demanded, stepping to face him. "We are no enemy, and bring dire word from Nalindor."

"The cataclysm of Nalindor is known to us," the other captain snapped. "And its instigators stand among you."

Vralsír turned to Silvanus in bewilderment.

"Seize them!"

Elves shoved their way into the grumbling company. Hands reached for Havarius, pulling his arms behind him as others stripped his sword from his belt. But neither he nor Silvanus struggled. The captain watched them, indignant. Without another word, hard gauntlets shoved Havarius forward, and the line of warriors filed into the glowing streets.

Havarius paced the warmly lit chamber, ignoring the beautifully carven chairs in the corner where Silvanus sat patiently. Hysteria threatened to explode if he didn't do something.

"You will wear a line in that rug if you do not relent, alenon," Silvanus gently chided him.

Havarius scowled. "What's going on?" he growled. "Why in Aldaria did they arrest us?"

"The Elves do nothing out of ignorance, nor with haste. We must wait and see what lies before us."

"They know about the Well, they know something terrible happened. Something we caused—"

"No," said Silvanus harshly. "We did what was necessary to protect Andaaya. The Elves shall hear our truth."

Havarius scoffed. "I'm not sure I know what's true anymore."

Silvanus sighed, shifting in his seat. "All will be made clear. We have not come this far to fall to fear or suspicion now."

Havarius stopped, swerving to face him and curling his hands into fists at his side. "No? Well, I don't know about you, but there's a whole lot of fear inside me right now! I just doomed our entire nation to a curse that turns people into monsters. I probably killed the herald of Elowë and damned myself for eternity. And to top it all off, I betrayed and abandoned the love of my life, leaving her to be ripped to shreds at the hands of those, those beasts!"

Rage and helplessness boiled inside him as he stood there, trembling. Havarius felt as if another man had replaced him, that the darkest parts of his being had rebelled and toppled all he believed true about himself. He was a traitor, a scandalous blood mage unworthy of loyalty or love.

Havarius crouched on the floor, covering his face. Tears formed in the corners of his eyes, and his breath came in ragged gasps.

"Havarius."

A gentle hand wrapped around his shoulder and Havarius flinched. He jerked his face upwards, wet streaks running through the grime on his cheeks. Silvanus gazed at him tenderly, and for the first time, Havarius noticed the tears hanging in the old mage's own eyes.

"Havarius, my son," Silvanus whispered. "There is much I have done in the name of our people. Both good and ill. None of us see all ends, save Elowë himself. But above all, I swore to your father I would do all in my strength to protect you. And I have tried to shield you from the worst of our plight. You are no monster, Havarius. This burden is not yours to carry, but mine, and I shall do all I can to free you from this guilt. Trust me, as your father did."

Havarius shuddered, rage swarming beside bitterness, shame, and pain at the thought of his father. "I don't know," he wheezed. "Right now, I'm not any better than those beasts of Nalindor."

"Trust me, Havarius."

A key jingled in the wooden door, causing them to leap to their feet. The door barreled open, followed by a set of grim Elvish warriors.

"Follow us."

Silvanus strode after the first without another word. Havarius stumbled after him, still sulking. They turned, following the bright hall of exquisite stone where tufts of foliage poked through wide openings to the quiet street below.

"Heran?" Silvanus gasped.

Havarius' gaze shot up. A man in light Oathsworn armor stood timidly between another set of Elves at the junction before them. He bowed, eying Silvanus awkwardly.

"Grandmaster Silvanus," Heran replied. "I am sorry, sir. I tried to get word to you, but the Elves seized us before I had the chance."

"What happened, Heran?"

The Elves nudged them on, forcing the group down the corridor.

"I'm not sure, sir. One moment, we were peacefully working on our research. The next, our Elvish colleagues had vanished. One of my scribes returned to our study moments before the soldiers, saying Nalindor had fallen and the Oathsworn were wanted."

"Why? What did they want with you?" Havarius asked, sauntering up next to the captain as he followed Silvanus. Silvanus nodded for Heran to continue.

"I, I'm not sure. They arrested us without any explanation. We haven't seen or heard anything beyond our own chambers since yesterday."

"And the research?" asked Silvanus in a low voice.

"With the Elves, somewhere, sir. They were inspecting the iluvashtin as I was taken away."

They turned another corner into a wider hall, flanked by great sculpted columns and gleaming fountains. At the far end, a set of doors waited, guarded by more Elves. The group moved forward as the doors opened and then were ushered into another chamber. A row of raised stone tables with matching seats curved along with the rounded walls at the far end, looming over the otherwise empty room, save a single door to their left. Moonlight filtered through the open arches and the thick canopy of branches above.

Havarius and the others moved to the center, and the guards retreated to the edge. The room was ominously silent, save for the rustling of leaves.

Suddenly, the door opened, and a woman entered. Havarius knew her immediately from her elegant emerald dress and piercing blue eyes. Two men in similarly striking clothing followed close behind, and together they took the seats above the Oathsworn.

"Councilor Livanya," Silvanus said, bowing low. Havarius and Heran did likewise.

"Grandmaster Silvanus," she responded shortly. Her hard gaze scanned the trio, and guilt rose once more in Havarius' gut.

"I believe there has been some misunderstanding," Silvanus continued. "We have come to Ostinlaë with dire news to—"

"We know why you have come, Eldvenir. News has already reached us."

"Then others have survived the disaster," said Silvanus, unperturbed. "Thank the Creator. You understand then, councilor, what we must do. We must prepare."

"The Mist-curse shall be addressed in due order," she replied icily. "You have been brought before the remaining council to answer for the atrocities at the Great Well."

"Atrocities?" Silvanus echoed. "By whose word and proof are we accused of such?"

Livanya glanced towards the open door as another woman entered. Havarius jaw nearly dropped to the floor. "*Caelia*!"

Havarius saw her face twitch, but she avoided his desperate stare. Caelia turned to the councilors, taking a seat near the end.

Havarius' heart nearly beat out of his chest and the room spun. *She's alive. Thank you Elowë, thank you.*

"Princess Caelia of the Firewalkers risked her life to bring tidings of the darkness over Nalindor," Councilor Livanya continued, "and of the Oathsworn's involvement in its inception. She has allowed her memories to be examined by this council, and all that befell has been made known."

Havarius gaped at Caelia, dumbstruck and more confused than ever.

Hurt and fury shone like daggers in Livanya's eyes as she bore into each of them. "*Silvanus.* The Oathsworn stand accused of the murder of countless innocents and the decimation of our homeland. You have betrayed the Oath and the Creator himself. What say you?"

The room was silent as a tomb as all eyes hovered on the inscrutable old mage. He stepped closer and cleared his throat.

"Great councilors and friends," Silvanus began, "for one hundred years, this war has ravaged Andaaya. Edros has sat abandoned, and the Mantle has lain dormant as fear and destruction consumed both our peoples. Even as the Oathsworn were pushed from our ancestral homes and into the strongholds of the north, ever we sought to contain the bloodlust of our enemy.

"So it was that here, at what should have been our most jubilant celebration, the plot against both Elves and Eldvenir was discovered. The joy of Dragon Day became the means of annihilation for all who opposed the dominion of Firelord Turgaen, even to the Everking himself."

The councilors flinched, frowning deeper at Silvanus.

"When I learned of the Firelord's intentions, I implored High King Fael to act," he continued somberly. "He would not. And so, as the betrayal was revealed, and the Everking fell, we escaped to the only power remaining that could halt the Firelord's new-found might."

"Except you and your accomplice resorted to the Path of Blood, seeking to take what was not yours," Livanya snapped. "You combined the dark arts of Kanuh with the purity of iluvasil, an unholy melding that has brought doom upon us all! Do not deny it, Silvanus, we have seen the memory. And now we learn another scheme persisted here within our very walls." She scowled at Heran, who shifted nervously. "What further darkness did you plan with the sacred iluvashtin?"

"All I have done has been for the sake of Andaaya," Silvanus rebutted defensively. "The Firewalkers aimed for nothing less than the genocide of your people, councilor, as they did mine. There was no other path left to us in our darkest hour."

Livanya stared at him, cold and unrelenting. "That judgment is not yours to pronounce. Not even we see all ends."

"Even so. I shall stand by my actions, esteemed councilors. Nothing less than the full peace and security of Andaaya compels me."

The councilors glanced at one another, frowning. Livanya sighed, closing her eyes as her lips grew tight.

"Grandmaster Silvanus," she said seriously, "while your centuries of steadfast friendship with the Elves are commendable, the flagrant disregard for your actions within Nalindor leave this council bereft of words. This egregious lack of foresight has just as much led to the destruction of the Elves as the Firewalkers intended. I fear there is no choice."

Dread grew in Havarius as Councilor Livanya sat back, weariness overcoming her immortal face. The guards shuffled closer. "For your betrayal against the Creator and the destruction of Nalindor, this council declares your Oath nullified. Never again shall we name you Eldvenir." Silvanus reeled as if he were gasping for breath.

Then she turned to Havarius. "Likewise, your accomplice, Ambassador Havarius Stormcrown, shall no longer be recognized among the Elf-kin for his actions before the Great Well." Havarius was too overwhelmed to feel anything but numb. His soul filled not with indignation, but shame, as he stared mutely at the floor.

"No," said Silvanus abruptly. "Councilors, the fault of the cataclysm—"

"Shall be borne by all who transgressed," Livanya finished. "This is our judgment. Captain Heran and his people we deem innocent in this matter. It is clear their obedience to your orders is separate from this striking offense. However, the device of the ancients and his research shall remain in our possession, as is our right as its makers."

She leaned closer. "Furthermore, the Elves shall uphold the sacredness of all life. Even in so great a sin, your lives are your own. As the power to strip the blessings of the Eldvenir lies solely with the Creator, imprisonment shall be your sentence. For this, the iluvashtin shall be your chains."

"Livanya..." Silvanus whispered.

"Silvanus, you shall spend ages unnumbered within the iluvashtin you concealed from this council, barred from this mortal realm. Only once the power of your iluvasil is spent shall you be free." Silvanus shuddered in horror. "A second vessel shall be commissioned immediately. Havarius Stormcrown shall bear his sentence upon its completion."

"No!"

All faces turned to the outburst from the corner, where Caelia stared wide-eyed at Livanya. The councilor looked at her, surprised. "Princess Caelia?"

"I, surely there is another way," she stammered, holding the sides of her arms. Havarius could tell she was trembling in her soft velvet dress.

Livanya studied her for several moments. "This council acknowledges the horrors thrust upon you, princess. You have lost much in these harrowing events. What sentence would you have the council consider?"

Caelia turned her attention upon Havarius. Shame, guilt, and desperation flooded his mind as he finally found her captivating gaze. Beyond her alarm, Caelia was unreadable.

Please, please forgive me, he cried, reaching out subconsciously through the Void. His plea met only an iron wall, unyielding and obscured. Caelia looked away.

"Exile."

Livanya's brows raised as the other councilors peered at her in astonishment. Havarius sank to his knees, as if punched in the stomach. He could not stand, could not breathe. His heart shattered alongside his entire world.

The Elves exchanged nods, looking down upon his broken form.

"Very well," said Livanya gravely. "Havarius Stormcrown, you are henceforth banished from the lands of Andaaya. Never again shall you return to these shores. Should you fail to heed this, your original punishment shall be exacted for your transgression against its people. The council has spoken."

Havarius was dimly aware of firm hands pulling him to his feet and guiding him from the chamber. Silvanus whispered something behind him, but he did not hear it. His mind barely functioned, his vision blurred. Trapped within his prison of despair, Havarius stumbled from the chamber as silent as the tears flowing from the Firewalker gazing after him.

Chapter 23
Exile

"Havarius."

Silence.

"Havarius, listen to me," Silvanus whispered, gripping the slender stone slats of the window separating the lavish rooms of their makeshift prison. Havarius sighed. "Please, our time grows short," he continued with a sense of urgency. "Once I enter the iluvashtin, I shall be unable to reach you. Listen to my words."

"Why?"

"Excuse me?"

Havarius forced his head to turn in the old mage's direction as he lay sprawled across the simple, yet elegant, bed. "It's over, Silvanus. We're finished, and Andaaya is doomed."

"Do not give up hope, not yet."

Havarius sat up, agitated. "It doesn't matter anymore. Caelia is gone. Today may be the last you see of the waking world, and I'll never lay eyes on my family or home again."

"We must warn the Oathsworn," Silvanus continued, ignoring him. "They will escort you past Captain Heran's chambers on the way to the docks. Please, you must get this into his hands." Silvanus pressed a small, leather-bound journal through the opening. Havarius stared at him. "It is a copy of his research. It must reach the others in Calharon before the Mist. They might still find a way to replicate our prototype in time."

Havarius didn't move. He continued staring at the wrinkled hand as Silvanus extended the book further. "I'm done, Silvanus. It's over."

"*Havarius*," Silvanus said sternly. "Come to your senses. This is no longer about us. What we can do, what we must do, is ensure the survival of the Eldvenir. Of Lina and your sister."

Havarius narrowed his eyes, bristling as he jumped to his feet. "You lied to me about Angoladan! You used my connection with Caelia for your own plans while leaving me in the dark. This is all your fault! You think I'm going to trust another one of your schemes?"

Silvanus winced, clearly hurt. "Havarius, I swear to you, I never intended for such pain to befall you. Were it I could remove you from this disgrace, I would give anything."

Havarius turned away from him, focusing on the empty corner at the foot of his bed.

"Right now, all that matters is saving what remains of our people," Silvanus murmured. "For Orian's sake, I must try to save your family. Please, Havarius, believe me."

Doubt wrestled with fear deep within him as he flinched at the mention of his name. Havarius trembled in rage, refusing to meet the pleading man's gaze.

"I'm sorry, Silvanus. I won't do it."

Footsteps rose from the corridor, and Silvanus slipped the notebook back into the folds of his robe.

"All that you have lost is my fault. I have failed you, Havarius," he whispered, his voice breaking. "Please, forgive me."

The door to Havarius' room opened and the Elvish guard stepped in, beckoning. As he walked into the hall, Havarius looked one last time into Silvanus' blue gaze, glistening with tears. "Goodbye, Silvanus."

Boots echoed in the silence as Havarius was swept from their chambers, never again to behold his master. Silvanus slumped onto the hard floor, letting his tears fall.

⸻ ◆ ⸻

Gulls cried over the crash of waves along the shore. The air was heavy with the smell of salt and brine of the sea. A deep bank of clouds covered the early morning sun, casting a gray tone over the quiet streets and quays of Ostinlaë. Havarius gazed absently at the intricate stone of the pier as the Elves led him past a fleet of majestic ships rocking gently in their moorings.

He glanced up as they slowed, startled to find Captain Vralsír waiting patiently before him. The guards bowed as they approached, then quietly withdrew towards the city.

"Vralsír?"

"Ma Elowë vesir nau oín, Havarius Stormcrown," the captain said, barely audible over the waves. "I shall escort you to your ship."

Havarius silently followed him to a small ship anchored at the very end of the dock. The first thing he noticed was the simple, unadorned prow. There was no Veil Beacon, no arcane device to guide the way back through the Veil enshrouding Andaaya from the rest of the world.

There would be no return.

Vralsír paused as they neared the ship, turning to face him. Havarius looked in wonder at the Elf's outstretched hands. Havarius' sword gleamed against the viridian gauntlets, the grime and damage of battle erased from its polished sheath.

"Edros is a dangerous place," said Vralsír, passing him the blade. "You shall need every gift and skill at your disposal."

"Thank you," he murmured, nodding with gratitude.

Vralsír studied him with a rueful look. "Listen to Elowë's voice within you. Let him guide your path. Should fate deem it, seek out my kindred at the Havens in Istwyneir. There, you may find shelter from the wildness of the Great Continent."

"Allovan'oín," Havarius replied with a bow. "I can never repay you for this kindness."

Vralsír smiled. "It is my pleasure. Më nala suilon vas basír, alenon." Then he stepped aside, retreating past the rows of silent, towering ships.

Havarius took a deep breath, stepping closer to his small vessel. He rounded the side of the small cabin at the aft, and froze. A small figure in a brown hooded cloak stood facing the lapping waves. Slowly, it turned, pulling back the hood. Soft, blonde waves spilled from the cover.

"Caelia?"

Her hard eyes cut into him as his heart leapt and trembled.

Havarius stumbled towards her, collapsing at her feet. "I'm so sorry. Caelia, I'm so, so sorry." Great sobs wracked his body and his breaths came in heaving gulps as he stared at the ground. "I betrayed you, betrayed your trust. You must hate me, and I deserve every ounce of it."

The words came spilling from his stuttering lips. "I, I ruined your life. I ruined our love. All of it is my fault. I am so desperately sorry for what I've done to you. Please, forgive me."

Hot tears splattered the deck as Havarius bowed lower, tremors consuming his hunched form. He shut his eyes, unable to even look at her simple leather boots.

Gentle hands met his shoulders. Havarius' head snapped up, splattering more tears across the boards. Her tender eyes, tinged with pain, lingered over his.

"You hurt me," she murmured, never leaving his gaze. "And I forgive you."

Havarius choked and wept harder. He felt unworthy of even her touch. "Why? I, I don't deserve it. I don't deserve you."

"No, you don't," she said softly. "Nor do I deserve you. You did what you thought would protect me. I don't fault you for that." A faint smile broke from her smooth lips. "Do you remember when I told you I loved you?"

He nodded, still struggling for breath, as the vision of that night within the garden filled his mind.

"I meant it. Unconditionally. I am free—of this war, of my father." Her delicate fingers quivered as they moved down his arms. "My love is mine to give to whom I choose. And I choose you, Havarius Stormcrown. Now, and forever."

His fingers interlocked with hers, his heart nearly bursting from his chest. Humility, gratitude, joy. Shame and guilt vanished as dew before the sun as new life filled his soul.

"I choose you, Caelia Urvos. Now, and forever."

Caelia pulled his shaking body from the deck, and he wrapped her in his arms. She rested her head against his, closing her eyes with a sigh.

"I love you," she whispered.

"I love you too."

He pressed his lips into hers, warmth tingling to the tips of his hands as the waves and world faded into obscurity. Caelia gazed at him with bright eyes, smiling. Havarius sighed, wiping away the damp on his cheeks with his soaked sleeve.

Caelia laughed. "You'll be wetter than a fish by the time we reach Edros."

"You're really coming with me?"

She gave him a playful shove. "Of course I am," she said matter-of-factly. Caelia sauntered to the bow and untied the rope. "I've never seen the Great Continent, you know, though I know all the stories." Havarius grinned, moving to untie the aft.

"Think of all the amazing places no one has ever seen!" Caelia continued excitedly. "I mean, Westrock and Hamidia are probably pretty boring. That's where everyone else went. But what about the north? Or the south? Oh! We could visit the Elves in Istwyneir!"

Havarius chuckled. "I might have a connection there."

They unfurled the sail, and the wind caught it. The small vessel slipped from the pier, racing quietly across the open sea.

"My father had several maps of the northern lands," Havarius added as he adjusted the sail. "When I was younger, he had these amazing stories from his tour on an island near the coast. Beautiful forests, sweeping plains, breathtaking mountains... Also, trolls. Maybe we avoid the trolls."

Caelia giggled as she tied her loose hair behind her. "It sounds thrilling. Even the trolls. In Sabron, we knew little about the north. What was it called, the island?"

"Karthmoor by the natives, I think."

"Huh." Caelia smiled at him. She moved closer, wrapping her arms over his shoulders, and his heart skipped a beat. "Maybe they would make good neighbors for our homestead?"

Havarius felt as if his grin couldn't possibly widen any further as he lost himself in her eyes. "Maybe so."

For a moment, a shifting gleam behind her drew his attention. He stared towards the sweeping hills fading rapidly beyond Ostinlaë. The gray clouds seemed... lighter. He squinted harder. There was a pale sheen to those nearest the land, the dark gray fading.

Caelia eyed him, confused. "What is it?" She turned to look.

Slowly, the clouds morphed from pale gray to a faint blue. Almost sickly.

The hue spread across the horizon, grasping hungrily towards the sky.

Caelia gasped. Havarius took a deep breath and gripped her hand tighter.

"Elowë, save us."

THE END

Thank You

Thank you for checking out *The Cataclysm*! If you enjoyed the story, would you help me out?

Ratings and reviews are one of the biggest ways you can help indie authors connect with more book lovers. The minute or two you take to add your thoughts on the story (or even just a couple seconds for a rating!) can make all the difference in how the algorithm shares it out

Leave a review!

with more curious readers. It also means the world to me! Pick your favorite place to review (Amazon, Goodreads, etc.), and thanks!

Join my newsletter!

Ready for the next book?
Something new is always on the horizon. Want to know when the next book in *The Oathsworn Chronicles* will arrive? Join other readers on the quest by using the QR code to the left or by going to www.zrmccormick.c om to learn more. My amazing sub-

scribers are always the first to hear the news about Kickstarter, new releases, and freebies.

Still want more?

Don't you hate when a story ends and there are still a dozen more places or things you wish you could explore? Me too. That's why I created a whole page of awesome bonuses for you to dive into while you wait for the next book! From high-resolution maps to

Explore the extras!

short stories to other exclusive content, go to www.zrmccorm ick.com/extras, or scan the QR code to the right to learn more about the world of *The Oathsworn Chronicles*!

Acknowledgments

This story was truly a joy to write, but wouldn't be what it is without the support of so many speaking insight and encouragement along the way.

First, I couldn't have asked for better beta readers. Ben and Lathem, you both tore through this story and offered a ton of brilliant questions and comments that really challenged me to improve. I can't thank you enough for dedicating your time to this book.

Daniel, thanks for designing such an amazing cover to truly complement the vision. I had very little to go on when we started, but you really nailed the elements that were hardest for me to articulate.

Most especially, Erica, for being my rock and encouragement in all the ups and downs. I couldn't have written this without your ability to keep our family afloat and giving me nights and weekends of writing along the way. Not only that, but you were always ready to be my sounding board and help me solidify the foundation for the series to come. (Seriously, for those of you who loved the ending, you have her to thank for it.)

Most of all, thank you, Jesus, for every step you've guided on this journey. Let my words stir hearts to see the whisper of your glory and love for us, our true Creator.

THE ALDARIAN COMPENDIUM

If, like the many others before, you've flipped or scrolled to the back of this story because you have no idea what that person just said or where in Aldaria they're at, welcome! Several of the Heraldan Collective's brightest minds have curated this appendix to help you keep everything straight. Within the Compendium, you will find terms listed alphabetically for ease of use. Bear in mind, several scribes continue to work on this ever-expanding tome. Be sure to check back as each new story is discovered!

Aldaria (ahl-DARE-ee-ah) - the planet and known mortal world

Alenon (AHL-eh-non) - my friend

Allovan'oín (ahl-oh-VON-oh-EN) - thank you (lit. my thanks to you)

Andaaya (an-DIE-ah) - the lost continent of the Elves and birthplace of the Oathsworn and Firewalker Orders; home to the first humans awakened by Elowë

Angoladan (an-GOHL-ah-don) - an immortal Void-wing and herald of Elowë; one of the dragons who traditionally visited Nalindor on Dragon Day

Aria Stormcrown - the sister of Havarius and daughter of Orian and Lina Stormcrown

Autumnhold - a large Oathsworn region and city in western Andaaya, recently overtaken by the Firewalkers

Avanuil (ah-VAHN-weel) - my lord or my king

Baldeira (bahl-DEER-ah) - a small Oathsworn city between Nalindor and Calharon

Caelia Urvos - the princess of the Firewalker Order and ambassador to the Elves; a powerful mage and first mortal to discover the ability of restorative blood magic

Calharon (cahl-HAR-uhn) - the largest city of the Oathsworn Order on Andaaya, far north of Nalindor

Captain Heran - an officer of the Oathsworn Order reporting directly to Silvanus

Captain Vralsír (vrahl-SEER) - an Elvish captain of Nalindor

Commander Marlond - a high-ranking Firewalker officer recently transferred from Dor Telmon to Nalindor

Councilor Livanya - the Elvish leader of Ostinlaë and advisor to High King Fael

Dor Telmon (TELL-men) - a Firewalker city south of Nalindor

Dragol Urvos (drah-GOAL) - the crown prince of the Firewalker Order; just as ruthless as his father, Turgaen; also extremely ambitious, seeking out forgotten secrets to increase his dominance

Dragon Day - an annual Elvish event commemorating the creation of Aldaria and the dragons who gave up their celestial status to bring about the mortal world

Dragon Tamers - an ancient sect of Firewalkers who used blood magic to enslave the dragons of Aldaria

Edros (EH-droas) - also known as the Great Continent; the largest known landmass in Aldaria and birthplace of modern mankind

Eldvenir (EHLD-vin-eer) - Oathsworn (see *Oathsworn Order*)

Elowë (EHL-oh-way) - the Creator (in Elvish); also referred to as the Creator in the modern era; the sole deity and maker of all things known and unknown

Evermont - a small Oathsworn city between Nalindor and Calharon

Firewalker Order - founded by Lornan and other Oathsworn cast from the Order for their use of blood magic and violent pursuit of power, Firewalkers are native humans of Andaaya who combine the intrinsic abilities of Andaayan mortals with blood magic; they primarily view the world though survival of the strongest and pride themselves on being the antithesis of the Oathsworn Order

Halls of Eternal Slumber - a sacred valley near the western coast of Andaaya, first inhabited by the Elves and later gifted to the Oathsworn for housing the iluvashtin

Havarius Stormcrown (ha-VAR-ee-us) - a member of the Oathsworn Order and native of Andaaya who becomes the Order's ambassador to the Elves during the Andaayan Civil War

Hennaleth (hen-ah-LITH) - elder tree; ancient trees brought by the Elves from the Ageless Realm; growth takes centuries, rising several stories high at full maturity, with exceptionally wide trunks and thick branches

High King Fael - one of the oldest of all immortal Elves who led his people from the Ageless Realm to Aldaria at its founding

Highwall - a small Oathsworn city between Reachwind Keep and Calharon

Iluvan (ih-LEW-vihn) - silver stone; blue-gray crystals found deep underground containing stores of magical energy

Iluvashtin (ih-lew-VASH-tin) - silver dream; a rectangular chamber of polished stone, glass, and metal powered by iluvan; known more recently as a "time pod" for its ability to provide suspended animation; knowledge of its construction, including its interior instruments and relationship to iluvan, was lost with the passing of the Elves

Iluvasil (ih-LEW-vah-sil) - silver star; also known as white iluvan; rare shards of pure white crystal brought by the Elves from the Ageless Realm; only form of iluvan capable of absorbing and storing nearly limitless quantities of magical energy

Iluvimír (ih-LEW-vih-meer) - silver mirror; large formations of iluvan that are shaped and tuned to respond to another through the lost arts of the Elves; allow instantaneous communication of sound and images

Kanuh (kah-NEW) - the Deceiver; a rebel Void-wing who persuaded other dragons to steal Elowë's power and refashion the mortal plane as he desired; after being cast beyond the Void, he discovered a way to communicate with and teach blood magic to the first Firewalkers

Karthmoor - a large island nation off the northern coast of Edros

Lendilmyne (lend-el-MEEN) - sun flower; flower with small, elongated, white petals with vibrant yellow streaks; found only near Elvish settlements and is said to be another item they brought to Aldaria from the Ageless Realm; rumored to possess powerful healing properties, from quickening healing to curing a variety of ailments

Lieutenant Jorin - an officer of the Oathsworn Order

Lina Stormcrown (LEEN-ah) - the wife of Orian Stormcrown and mother of Havarius

Lornan - an Oathsworn warrior seduced by Kanuh into learning blood magic; he and his disciples were cast from the Order and went on to found the Firewalker Order in response

Ma Elowë vesir nau oín (MAH EHL-oh-way veh-SEER NOW oh-EN) - may the Creator smile upon you; a customary Elvish greeting

Më nala suilon vas basír (MAY na-LAH swee-LAHN VAS ba-SEER) - let joy mark our farewell; a customary Elvish farewell

Nalindor (nah-LIN-dohr) - the largest city in Andaaya and the capital of the Elves, known for its magnificent architecture and natural beauty; home to the largest Elvish population in Aldaria

Oathsworn Order - an order founded by the first men of Andaaya who embraced faith in Elowë and the Elves' teaching on the Mantle of Stewardship; members of the Order undergo a secretive ceremony bestowing enhanced magical abilities and lifespans

Oín su remon (oh-EN SOO ree-MON) - you are welcome

Orian Stormcrown (ore-EE-in) - the ambassador to the Elves for the Oathsworn Order as well as its former warden-commander; also the father of Havarius, instructing him in the politics of Andaaya

Ostinlaë (ah-STIN-lay) - an Elvish city on Andaaya's eastern coast

Reachwind Keep - the traditional capital of the Oathsworn Order in western Andaaya, first founded by the Elves

Sabron (sah-BRON) - the capital city of the Firewalker Order on Andaaya, far southwest of Nalindor

Silvanus Aerulion (sil-VAHN-us air-ROOL-ee-in) - Grandmaster of the Oathsworn Order and native of Andaaya; seeks to end the Firewalkers' power by any means necessary

The Bound - immortal dragons and first creations of Elowë who gave up their ability to traverse the Void in order to take part in crafting the mortal plane; were forever bound to physical existence in Aldaria as part of their sacrifice

The Current - the lifeblood of magic in Aldaria; an unseen force mages tap into with their consciousness, releasing their abilities; a direct result of the Creator's Song, and a constant force underneath the physical world connecting everything together, no matter the distance or position in the Void

Troll - extremely large, vicious creatures found throughout northern Edros; tend to inhabit mountainous or densely forested regions where their thick gray or brown hides easily camouflage with the terrain; semi-intelligent but have no known speech

Turgaen Urvos (tur-GAIN) - the Firelord of the Firewalker Order and rival to Silvanus; known for his ruthlessness and cunning

Ventari Mountains (vehn-TAR-ee) - a range of high mountains in central Andaaya

Void-wing - immortal dragons and first creations of Elowë who did not pass into the mortal plane at its founding; retain the ability to traverse all planes of existence, though are rarely seen in the mortal world

Warden Karrick - a leader of the Oathsworn Order responsible for its eastern front in the Andaayan Civil War

Warden Sophia - a leader of the Oathsworn Order responsible for its western front in the Andaayan Civil War

Warden-Commander Gorim - the second-in-command of the Oathsworn Order under Silvanus

Year of Remembrance - a yearlong Elvish festival commemorating the creation of Aldaria and various important events in their efforts to cultivate Aldaria according Elowë's command

About the Author

Have you ever imagined exploring another universe?

When Z.R. McCormick outgrew his childhood of cloaks, wooden bows, and plastic swords (which were likely burned to the joy of his neighbors and their landscaping), that wonder inspired by stories of the fantastical was never quite left behind.

He began voyages into the world of Aldaria in between a career in IT, enjoying time with his beautiful wife, and chasing his own rambunctious younglings, culminating in his debut novel, *The Oathsworn Chronicles: Awakening,* released in late 2025. But until that darkness in Aldaria is vanquished, Z.R. is content to read about someone else's adventures with a cold brew and a cozy chair, which, as you might agree, is rather sensible.

Find out more about Z.R. and the world of Aldaria by visiting him at www.zrmccormick.com.

www.ingramcontent.com/pod-product-compliance
Lightning Source LLC
Chambersburg PA
CBHW031038310726

48969CB00007B/2034